ACCID

There was a hu— —ce
technicians, my film company colleagues,
village residents were all wandering in,
alarmed and demanding information. Pedestrians were peering in through the windows.

"They are not used to murder here in the village," Inspector Lucas commented to us. "It has not been since 1971 that one occurred—a German tourist, I believe."

"No, not true," I corrected him. "There was a murder only a few days ago."

"Do you mean here, madame?" he asked me incredulously.

"Yes, I do. Near the church outside of the village."

"If you are speaking of Madame Dodd, she was killed in an automobile accident. It may have been a preventable one. But nonetheless an accident."

"No," I insisted. "Murder."

A CAT WITH NO REGRETS

An Alice Nestleton Mystery

by
Lydia Adamson

A SIGNET BOOK

SIGNET
Published by the Penguin Group
Penguin Books USA Inc., 375 Hudson Street,
New York, New York 10014, U.S.A.
Penguin Books Ltd, 27 Wrights Lane, London W8 5TZ, England
Penguin Books Australia Ltd, Ringwood, Victoria, Australia
Penguin Books Canada Ltd, 10 Alcorn Avenue, Toronto, Ontario,
Canada M4V 3B2
Penguin Books (N.Z.) Ltd, 182–190 Wairau Road,
Auckland 10, New Zealand

Penguin Books Ltd, Registered Offices:
Harmondsworth, Middlesex, England

First published by Signet, an imprint of Dutton Signet, a division
of Penguin Books USA Inc.

First Printing, May, 1994
10 9 8 7 6 5 4 3 2 1

The first chapter of this book was previously published in *A Cat in a Glass House.*

Printed in the United States of America

PUBLISHER'S NOTE:
This is a work of fiction. Names, characters, places, and incidents either are the product of the author's imagination or are used fictitiously, and any resemblance to actual persons, living or dead, events, or locales is entirely coincidental.

BOOKS ARE AVAILABLE AT QUANTITY DISCOUNTS WHEN USED TO PROMOTE PRODUCTS OR SERVICES. FOR INFORMATION PLEASE WRITE TO PREMIUM MARKETING DIVISION, PENGUIN BOOKS USA INC., 375 HUDSON STREET, NEW YORK, NEW YORK 10014.

1

Wouldn't you know that the one thing to come along and ruin a perfect trip would be my crazy cat Pancho.

There I was, seated sumptuously in a *private jet*. On the last leg of a seven-hour flight from New York to Marseilles. I'd never been there before, but I just knew it was going to be singularly . . . atmospheric. And so I sat there luxuriating in the huge leather seat, the engines humming quietly somewhere in the sleek steel bird's belly. By turns, I sipped my chi-chi mineral water and dozed—my dreams full of muscular little Frenchmen and long-legged ladies apache dancing; miscellaneous scenes from the musical *Fanny*; and the best fish soup in the whole wide world.

But the story gets even better than that. I was on my way to become a movie star! I'd actually landed a featured part in a thriller that was being shot in southern France.

Up ahead of me, in a black wool Calvin Klein that had set her back four figures, was Dorothy Dodd, who was bankrolling the film. At her right hand was her young lover, Ray Allen Penze, the star of the venture. On the seats across from them were three cat carriers, each holding one of Dorothy's beautiful Abyssinian cats.

In the row behind them, a small mountain of plastic martini glasses on his fold-down tray, was Sidney Rice, the gentle, fine British actor who would play the other male lead.

Then there was ebullient Brian Watts, the producer who had hired me. Accompanying him was Cilla Hood, Brian's recently acquired bedmate, a beautiful, youngish blonde whom he had met only a few months before at a New York party and promised an unforgettable trip to the south of France. Well, he hadn't been far off the mark on that one.

It all seemed impossibly glamorous: an entire, fabulously appointed jet hired just to carry five people and five cats across the Atlantic. As my old friend Anthony Basillio might put it, Dorothy Dodd was no piker.

Wait a minute . . . correction . . . *six* people. I forgot to include myself in the tally. Me: the female lead, "the woman," the final principal in this three-character epic *The Emptying*. The whole show would be placed in the hands of Claude Braque, one of the more prestigious second-string European directors.

The money they offered me was incredible . . . by my standards, anyway. And the last concession they made to me sealed my participation—they said I could bring along my cats. Which brings me back to Pancho.

The first six hours of the flight had been delightfully restful. That quiet time had helped me to recover from the last two insane weeks in New York, during which I had experienced what could only be called a spending frenzy. I'd spent damn near fourteen solid days shopping. The $19,500 advance I received, after agent's commission, had unhinged me. That was more money than I'd ever seen at one time in my life. I wined and dined Basillio royally, I bought gifts for my neighbor Mrs. Oshrin and my girlfriends, lavished toy mice and gourmet fish on my cat-sitting charges. And I nearly cleaned out the fancy Madison Avenue pet boutiques with things for my own felines, Bushy and Pancho. As for the things I purchased for myself . . . I'm simply too embarrassed to go over the list. Oh, what a glorious time I was having.

So, even though I usually hate flying, this trip was a day at the beach. And then Pancho struck.

According to the captain—I guess that's what the person ferrying the six of us was called—we were about an hour out of Marseilles. I thought the cats deserved a treat for being so cooperative, sitting patiently in their little mobile prisons. So I retrieved the plastic bag full of dried liver snaps and opened Bushy's carrier to give him a few. The big

Maine coon threw me a martyred look, but he took the snap.

Then I began gingerly to push one in through the grille of Pancho's box. At just that moment he banged his head heavily against the cell door. The clasp popped open and out flew Pancho.

Out flew my half-tailed, battleship-gray, paranoid mongrel—starting the lunatic run of his life—leaping from seat to luggage rack and back again—clawing at upholstery and throwing himself against the windows—a one-cat tornado. All accompanied by startled shrieks and curses from the other passengers.

"Pancho!" I screamed as he disappeared up the aisle. *"Please!"*

Silence.

Then the loudspeaker in the cockpit went on and we heard a booming male voice, full of panic and rage: "Hey! Out there—hey! Someone come and get this damn cat out of here!"

I raced into the pilot's cabin. Pancho was sitting calmly atop the blinking control panel, daintily making his toilette.

The copilot looked blackly at me and began in a low, threatening tone, "If you don't get the—"

I grabbed Pancho by one of his wet paws and made my way swiftly back to my seat. I could hear Dorothy cooing placatingly to her three cats, still in their carriers. Pancho gave me little trouble going back inside his cell. "You little criminal," I whispered, "this is the last time you'll ever leave Twenty-sixth Street."

* * *

Marseilles was cold, but it wasn't like a New York February. There was moisture in the cool air, a reminder in the wind that the sea was nearby. After a perfunctory inspection at Customs we were ushered out of a side door at the airport, where two spanking new rented Volkswagen vans awaited.

Director Claude Braque was driving one of them. He was a tall, craggy man with healthy-looking, wavy hair; I recognized him immediately, noting that he was wearing the same safari jacket I'd seen in photos of him. The driver of the other vehicle was a young woman. Wearing jeans and a storm coat, she introduced herself as "Alison." Her blond hair was held back with a series of Chinese combs, and she wore a pair of those stylish sunglasses with midnight-black lenses.

The moment they spotted us they stepped out of their respective vans. *"Bienvenu!"* Braque called to us. "Welcome to France."

The young woman produced a bottle with the unmistakable orange Veuve Cliquot label and distributed paper cups all around. Braque expertly maneuvered the cork out of the chilled bottle and we all sipped. I drank mine, cringing at the "Hollywood" spectacle we were making. Clearly we would not be allowed to leave until the bottle was empty. I wondered if someone would be delegated to smash the empty against the fender of the nearest vehicle.

"Ridiculous!" I heard a minute later. I turned

to see Brian Watts, who had spoken, a few feet away. *What's ridiculous?* I wondered. *The champagne? The movie we were about to make?* But then I realized he was speaking to Dorothy Dodd, who stood next to her young lover, Ray Allen. A few words I couldn't hear were exchanged between the three of them. And then Ray Allen impulsively took Dorothy in his arms and planted a long, lingering kiss on her mouth. Well, I thought, perhaps some would think that kind of display was ridiculous, but I had done more foolish things than that in the recent past—when I'd had the mixed blessing of being in love with a younger man.

The shouting resumed a minute later. It seemed that Dorothy wanted to drive one of the vans herself, and Brian and Ray Allen were opposed to it. Miss Dodd, however, won the day. She was the boss, after all. She was paying for everything. I watched her climb into the Volkswagen.

Off we went—Dorothy in the lead car, at the wheel. Next to her was Ray Allen Penze. Sidney Rice and Claude Braque, who presumably would be directing Dorothy to the village where we were staying, sat in back.

I was in the second van, seated next to Cilla Hood. Brian took the passenger seat next to the pretty blond production assistant.

Our destination was the small seacoast village of Ste. Ruffin, located in southwestern Provence, in the Camargue. It was a fascinating if little known part of the country—a large area of grassy plains, salt marshes, and dunes, where the tributaries of the Rhone reached the sea.

We hadn't gone many miles west from Marseilles when our surroundings began to undergo a transformation. Soon we were driving through a terrain that seemed to belong more to some remote archipelago than to Europe. There seemed to be a complete absence of green in the landscape. The winter wind, the legendary mistral, blew steadily—not freezing but relentless—though the sun was breaking brilliantly above us.

"Obviously, this is *not* high season in the Camargue," Cilla observed.

I thought she was merely making an observation, but Brian took it as an attack on him. "That's the reason we got the permits to shoot in Ste. Ruffin," he said roughly. "Because the tourist season is spring and fall. The village will be empty now. That's why we were able to rent the whole inn for twenty-one days, for a tenth of the usual nut." He seemed to grow more and more angry. "Besides that, winter light is *unbelievable* here! Arles is only a few miles north. Why do you think Van Gogh went there—for the fish soup?"

The van slowed down precipitously. We were all being jerked about, including my cats, who seemed to have accepted their fate—I didn't hear a peep from them.

"Sorry," Alison said, adjusting her glasses. "The other van keeps speeding up and then slowing again."

"What the hell is she doing—sightseeing?"

Brian said. He peered ahead at the other car. "And what the hell *is* she seeing?" he added, a note of worry in his voice. "She's got her rearview mirror turned down."

"Would you mind closing your window, Brian?" Cilla asked evenly. "I'm getting cold."

He rolled the window up a few inches, but not enough to cure the problem. The wind continued to rake us in back. Brian was a lovely man, but sometimes he could be difficult.

I had been told there were loads of horse farms in the Camargue. In fact, a bawdy acquaintance of mine had told me that a pampas cowboy was probably just what I needed at this time in my life. I was keeping half an eye out, but I didn't see anything that looked like a French wrangler about.

Soon enough, we all tired of the scenery, or the lack thereof. I closed my eyes, but I wasn't sleeping. Just reflecting on the sheer absurdity of it all. About ten hours ago I was in my pajamas, drinking coffee from my favorite cup and looking out my window at the out-of-business housewares store. Now I was in the French countryside thinking about lonesome cowboys. It *did* seem wrong, somehow, that you could get to the other side of the globe in less than half a day.

And something else seemed absurd: how, for all these years, I'd had the temerity to spurn virtually any stage role that did not come up to my bizarre, rarefied standards—yet I leapt at the chance to do what was probably going to be a stinker of a movie. Was it the money? Yes and no. Was it that I felt it was high time for me to be recognized on the street by the general public? Well, yes and no. Was it that I needed to get away from Manhattan? Yes.

"Will it be much longer?" I heard Brian ask our driver.

"No," said Alison. "We're very close now. Soon you'll see a small church with a low wall in front. It comes up suddenly. We just take a sharp left, and in a few minutes we'll be on the main street."

"Where the Ste. Ruffin marching band will play us into town," Cilla quipped mockingly. But Brian was too preoccupied to share the joke.

"Here it comes," said Alison.

I opened my eyes. The squat little church with its white stone wall was gorgeous.

"And here's where we make the turn," the young woman said confidently.

I reached out instinctively to steady the cats in their carriers.

But the van in front of us did not turn left. And it did not slow down at all. It accelerated! And a second later slammed into the stone wall with sickening force.

The four of us sat in the van for a few awful seconds, not knowing what to do. Then Brian was jumping from the car and running, yelling back to us as he moved, "Hurry!"

Cilla was the first to obey. She threw open

her door and began running toward him, crying all the while.

The front of the van was decimated.

Ray Allen Penze had been thrown from the vehicle and was on all fours on the ground. He was dazed, babbling—"Accidents will happen," was what he was saying, I think. Still, he seemed essentially unhurt.

Sidney Rice had landed between the seats. I could hear him breathing, but he was not moving at all.

Claude was sitting erect on the back seat, looking extremely alert, if haunted. He stared expressionlessly at us through the rear window, shaking his head ever so slightly. Then he sighed once.

Dorothy obviously had not been wearing her seat belt.

She had gone right through the windshield, so that half her body lay on the crumpled hood, the other half snagged grotesquely on the wheel inside.

The jagged windshield had very nearly severed her head. Her lifeless eyes stared straight ahead, past the wall, to the old church beyond.

Brian seemed mesmerized by the dangling head. He was pulling me toward it, though I don't know when it was that he'd taken hold of my hand, and I was resisting his tugs.

Finally bursting into action, Alison raced back to our van and roared off toward the village.

"She's going for help," Brian explained—

needlessly. "I know what happened," he added, sounding fevered.

Cilla and I turned to him.

"*I* know what it was," he went on. "She went for the brake and hit the accelerator instead. She wanted to brake for the turn . . . and instead her . . . her . . . she hit the gas and . . . "

Brian's face was clown-white. I thought he might faint. But he didn't. He exploded in tears. "My God! One tiny mistake! One wrong step—just one . . . "

It was then that I remembered Dorothy's animals—the Abyssinians. I rushed around to the back of the van and wrested open the hatchback. One of the carriers lay on its side. The others had gone sliding, and now rested at crazy angles to each other. I pulled out all three, set them carefully on the ground, and, one by one, cracked open the deluxe, velvet-lined cages to look in on the occupants.

I was not personally acquainted with these three beauties, but I knew the meaning of the sounds they were making: *feed me . . . now*. I knew that as long as they were hungry, they'd be fine. It was only their mistress—our benefactor, the impeccably dressed, reed-thin, outrageously rich, very dead Dorothy Dodd—who would never be hungry again.

2

It was so strange, the time after Dorothy Dodd's death. I sat in my lovely cottage with my suitcases and my cats. Oh, what a lovely cottage it was, built in the *cabane* style—a two-room, white-walled affair with thatched roof, like the herdsmen of old once lived in. But this was a modern version with plumbing and electricity.

Dorothy Dodd was not sitting in her deluxe *cabane*. She was in the morgue. Sidney Rice, Claude Braque, and Ray Allen Penze were all in the hospital.

I wasn't sure what I should be doing with myself. So I just sat there and watched Bushy and Pancho carrying out their minute inspection of the new surroundings. Somehow, it seemed inappropriate to throw myself into unpacking and settling in just yet.

What *does* a forty-one-year-old struggling stage actress who's on the brink of movie stardom do at a time like this? I decided to deal with my character. What else could I do? After all, I didn't know how closely Dorothy was entwined in the production. Would the shooting go on as scheduled? Or would it be put on hold? Or accelerated? Had Dorothy relegated the control of the purse strings to someone trustworthy? There were too many questions and no answers. I had to do the "show biz" thing.

The movie, I knew, was going to be an unbearably arty thriller. All kinds of alienation and pregnant silences and water lapping mercilessly against the rocks. A lot of sound and fury and cryptic glances signifying nothing.

But to be fair, the plot wasn't all that bad. It went like this: During the waning years of the cold war, a British Intelligence agent retires to a small village on the southern French coast after being crippled in a clandestine, CIA-sponsored operation in East Germany. The agent has threatened to write a tell-all memoir unless the CIA compensates him for his wounds. Unknown to him, a fugitive young IRA terrorist is hiding out in the village under an assumed name. The CIA sends a woman agent to the village to offer the Englishman one million dollars as a settlement. The Englishman wants more. The woman is ordered to terminate him. Loath to do it, she discovers the young terrorist, seduces him, and brings the two men together, believing that the Irishman will be forced to do her job for her.

No, not a bad plot. And I was to play the CIA

agent—the reluctant assassin. The problem was, I didn't have much clue who she was—intellectually or culturally. Was she a Dietrich, smoldering, ironic? Was she Garbo, slithering and lethal? Or was she a Jean Arthur all-American girl patriot?

I didn't know what kind of woman the writer had envisioned. I had never met him and you sure couldn't tell from the script. More to the point, what kind of woman did Braque, the director, want me to be? Being French, he might echo what Jacques Tourneur had said to Jane Greer when they were rehearsing for his film noir *Out of the Past.* "Do you know," he asked her, "what means *'impassif'*? This is what I want."

Oh, Braque would tell me what he wanted soon enough. Probably after the first take. I really didn't want that to happen. I just don't ever seem to get along with directors.

So I sat contemplating all those show business trifles, in my elegant little cottage. But even that task was too much for me. I wasn't hungry. I wasn't thirsty. I was just bone-tired.

I ended up brushing Bushy's coat. That is often what I do when I am at odds and ends. The long, languorous strokes of the grooming brush lulled me, made me even more tired, and a few seconds after he slipped from my grasp, I was fast asleep.

I woke with a start in the blue-black night. I had no idea where I was for a few awful seconds. Then I became aware of the insistent knocking at the cottage door. I fumbled about, banging into valises and cats, until I finally located the light switch.

When I opened the door an anxious Cilla Hood was standing there.

"Brian's back," she said rapidly. "He wants you—us—all over at the main house."

"Now?"

"Now," she repeated. "Right now." And that said, she trotted off to the next cabin.

I turned to find Bushy and Pancho both staring resentfully at me. I had forgotten to feed them!

"Sorry, fellas," I called out, rushed to my bags, and popped open two cans of choice tuna delight, leaving them on the floor. I filled the glass soap dish with dry food. Then I filled a paper cup from the dispenser in the bathroom with water. Off I went.

The main house of the inn was in the geographic center of the circle of cottages. It contained a lounge, a bar, a dining room, and the administrative office of the hotel.

They were waiting for me: Brian Watts and Cilla, Claude Braque and Ray Allen Penze. The latter two sported minor bruises and Ray had a dressing on one cheekbone.

"What about Sidney?" I asked Brian.

"They wouldn't release him yet. Said he may have some internal injuries. They need to run some tests."

We were seated on low rustic sofas that looked to be the French equivalent of the Adirondack style. On a gnarled wood table in front of us was a carafe of coffee along with a plate of sweets. I wondered if I'd slept through dinner.

Brian leaned forward and clasped his hands like a minister about to address the flock.

"Well," he started wearily, "it's a mess, isn't it? A real mess. But listen to me. This bloody film is going to get made. Do you know why?" He paused, milking the drama from the silence. "Because Dot would have wanted it that way."

Again he paused. He seemed to be waiting for a response from us. But no one said a word. "Well," he demanded finally, "do you all agree?"

We all nodded yes.

"Very well . . . Now, I don't know when Sidney is getting out of hospital. Let's figure two days time. What we have to do is get up a revised shooting schedule. Claude and I have started in on that already. But it's been a helluva long day. I want us all to meet here tomorrow morning at six-thirty for breakfast. Agreed?"

As all heads again bobbed assent, I looked over at Claude Braque. He had such a faraway look in his eyes, as if he might still be in shock, he could have been agreeing to anything.

"Okay. That's the ticket," Brian said. "Oh, one other thing—for what it's worth. The police are treating the accident as a DWI case."

"DWI?" It was Ray Allen Penze who'd asked

the question. "Does that mean the same thing as in the States? Like you're drunk?"

"Yes," Brian said, "exactly the same thing."

"Are they serious!"

"Quite serious," Brian replied, holding up his hands. "I know . . . I know. Of course I argued with them. I told them Dorothy had had nothing but a single cup of champagne at the airport. The officer I spoke with admitted that she didn't necessarily have to be legally drunk. But he said she was a fool because she gulped alcohol after a seven-hour flight and then got behind the wheel of a strange car to drive a dangerous, unfamiliar road. There was nothing I could say. Anyway, I called her family in Georgetown. They're flying over here. They want to cremate the body and spread the ashes somewhere in a little town in Provence. I don't remember the name. They said it was a wish Dorothy had expressed long ago."

We sat without speaking, glumly pinned to our seats until Brian spoke again. "That's it then. Chins up."

"Anyone care for a brandy?" Cilla Hood asked, heading for the bar.

I didn't. I said good night to the group and headed back to my room.

I closed the cottage door quietly behind me. A feeling of utter lostness had descended on me, swiftly and undeniably. For the first time, I felt myself truly to be a stranger in a strange land. And all I had to help me out was an outdated French phrase book with a rudimentary grammar.

But then I saw his royal highness Maine coon cat Bushy stretched out on my bed. And I laughed out loud. France didn't mean a damn thing to Bushy. He would take over my bed even if I were in a harem in old Baghdad.

But where was dear deranged Pancho?

I found him in the bathroom, perched on the ledge where tub met back wall. He looked most confused and unhappy. I sat across from him on the far ledge of the tub and inquired what was bothering him. He was silent. Pancho rarely answered questions. But, from the furtive looks he was casting out, I had a good idea what was going on. Pancho was trying to decide if his unknown and unseen enemies had followed him over the ocean.

After all, in Manhattan he spent his entire day fleeing from those imaginary enemies, who were always half a step behind him. He was a stranger in a strange land, too, and he must have been worried that "they" were hot on his trail, about to break into the cottage at any moment, or maybe already here.

Pancho didn't want to be comforted. I didn't know how to help him, so I let him be.

As for me, it was time to unpack. I emptied my bags and surveyed all the things I'd brought along. All the critical and totally useless effects that define me and my cats. I hung the clothes and stashed the toiletries and found spaces for the knickknacks. Then I changed into one of my new nighties and went to bed.

But, to quote the country-western song, sleep wouldn't come.

I'm no stranger to insomnia, but unlike most people I divide my bouts with it into good insomnia—lying awake for hours thinking—and bad insomnia—agitated tossing and turning, or making too many trips into the kitchen for too many chocolate cookies. This one was bad. Between the strange effects of jet lag and the fact that I'd already slept earlier in the evening, I realized just how long a night I was facing.

That's when I got my brilliant idea to take the cats outside—to give them their first real look at France.

Back in New York, I do take Bushy out once in a while, but never Pancho. He is too unpredictable . . . too crazy.

And now I was prepared for such an adventure, because in my preflight shopping frenzy I had purchased two fancy cat harnesses. I slipped one on the ever-wary Pancho without too much of a fight from him. The three of us were ready for our nocturnal adventure.

The cats were remarkably calm. All they did was amble about and sniff at the ground. It was a warm night for winter. The moonlight was very bright.

Bright enough to see the hulking wreck of the van that had carried Dorothy to her death.

It had obviously been towed back here and was now resting beside its healthy twin.

I picked up Pancho in my arms and walked slowly over to the van. There was still blood on the smashed window and hood.

There was something academic about the scene—as if I were looking at a painting entitled "Human Blood Over Glass." For the first time since the accident I really began to think about it. And there were things that deserved thinking about.

Why would a sharp, no-nonsense woman like Dorothy drive a vehicle without adjusting the driver's side rearview mirror . . . as Brian had pointed out on the ride from the airport.

And why hadn't she worn her seat belt? It probably would have saved her life.

Dorothy had once been named Woman Entrepreneur of the Year. She had made and lost and then recaptured fortunes in the magazine and communications industries. She was daring but she had also been careful.

I walked closer to the bloody windshield.

I noticed a strange thing. At first I thought it was an optical joke being played by the moon. But no.

On the remnants of the front window were bluish smeary streaks of treated water—the universally known cleanser for windshields. As if Dorothy had been driving in the rain, used her wipers, and then cleaned the windows after the downpour. But how could that be? I was in the van right behind her. There had been no rain. The skies had remained perfectly clear and the windshield on the other car was spotless.

Pancho suddenly squirmed out of my grasp and leapt onto the hood of the wrecked van, and then onto the good one. I heard that hideous sound of kitty retching, and looked down to see that Bushy had helped himself to some nearby weeds.

Insomnia or no, it was time to get back to the cottage.

3

It was a lovely place to have breakfast, sitting at the rustic round table in the dining room with the strong winter sun filling the room. Friends had told me that the French weren't very much on breakfast—a baguette with a little butter, perhaps a croissant, and coffee. But apparently the inn had anticipated the American preoccupation with the morning meal. There was orange juice on the table, and fresh fruit and yogurt and sliced ham, along with the warm croissants and piping hot coffee. The staff was taking good care of the guests—those of us who had survived the trip here.

Ray Allen Penze and Claude Braque were already eating lustily when I arrived. I tried to catch up with them. But Brian Watts, who had called the early morning meeting, was nowhere in sight. Nor was Cilla.

I was enjoying another spoonful of apricot jam when the production assistant, the young woman who had driven our van, entered the room and took the chair next to mine. She was again wearing jeans and dark glasses.

"I think I should formally introduce myself, Miss Nestleton," she said to me.

"Alice," I corrected.

She smiled prettily and repeated my name: "Alice. Thank you. My name is Alison Chevigny. It's sort of similar to yours, isn't it?"

It was my turn to smile. Then I passed her the basket of croissants.

At that moment one of the waitresses passed the table and asked something in French. Alison responded without hesitating in fluent French. This Alison was no doubt valuable. Not only competent at her job but fluent in at least two languages. I couldn't really determine what nationality she was.

I caught Braque looking at me. He turned away quickly. I smiled into my coffee. It was the old cat and mouse game between director and actress. We both knew that sooner or later we'd be squaring off. Probably sooner rather than later. But we were avoiding each other for the moment. We were gathering our strength, laying up our ammunition, each trying to look more professional than the other, but at the same time more compassionate and perceptive.

Then Cilla Hood burst into the room and began breathlessly to address us en masse, as if she were bringing the troops a dispatch from the front. "Brian . . . will not be here this morning. He's been called away to Marseilles on important business. I don't know what it is. All I know is that the owner of the inn woke him at three this morning with an urgent message from the American Consulate and Brian took off in the van a couple of hours later."

What a strange little speech. A bit threatening. A bit mysterious. No one knew quite how to respond.

Finally, Braque spoke in his deeply accented tone, almost a parody of a sexy Frenchman's voice. "Well," he said slowly, "I think we have just been given a day off."

When breakfast was over I decided it was time for me to start playing the proverbial tourist. I had read my Michelin and was ready for my first walking tour of the village of Ste. Ruffin. I knew what the place was all about in theory. It used to be a fishing village. But no longer. Only a few vessels still tied up at the harbor. The town now lived on the tourist trade, but that was mainly from spring through early fall. In February, according to the guide, its charm was different, because the only people around were the hard-core inhabitants—the baker, the butcher, the retired fishermen, the priest, and a few artists who have adopted the place as their own.

After returning to the cottage to feed my friends, I changed into my tourist tweeds and sturdy shoes and set out for the real world. I was eager for as much charm as the little town could muster up.

I wasn't disappointed. Ste. Ruffin was

lovely. One long main street dotted with shops as well as sturdy little shuttered houses, and three cross streets bisecting it. There was a café in one corner of the square, a church with a mighty steeple in another corner, a few retail shops, a patisserie, a tobacconist, and what seemed to be a general store, selling everything from dust mops to postcards.

Before I knew it I was on the wharf. It was a glorious morning, the sharp wind whipping in off the Rhone. And there was that marvelous sunlight everyone talked about. I could look at my hands and actually see my skin. I mean, the way it really is.

"Good morning."

It was a shock to hear that greeting in English. At first I thought I'd imagined it. But then I saw a woman waving at me gaily. She was behind one of the corroded wharf poles, and her rust-colored beret seemed to meld with the pole. She was seated at an easel facing the water.

I returned her greeting and walked over to her. I looked down at her work. She was painting the endless horizon.

The woman was in her early fifties, a bit plump, and she wore a bulky tan sweater over flannel slacks. Her hair was unkempt beneath the hat—wildly curly black with gray. She had a wonderful, open face.

"You must be making the film here."

"Yes, that's right."

"And you are an actress, no?"

"Yes, I am. I'm Alice Nestleton."

"How do you do, Alice. I am Suzanne Aubert."

"It's so kind of you to speak English with me," I said tentatively, "but you're not . . . English, are you?"

She laughed. A laugh I wish I possessed. "I worked for many years in Canada. Quebec. It was a French bank, but we had many English-speaking clients . . . many Americans."

"Your English is excellent."

"I enjoy speaking it. It's been a long while."

"Do you live here all year round?"

"Oh, yes. My husband and I came here ten years ago. But he is dead now. Now I am alone. And I paint every day. Except when it rains. I love to paint the sea. But sometimes I just turn"—and she did so in illustration—"and paint the village." She laughed girlishly at her own simplistic description.

We fell silent then and I stood there beside her for the longest time, watching her work.

After a time she said without turning: "I have heard of the terrible death."

"Yes, it was terrible. And there was no reason for it."

She began methodically to clean her brushes. "Will you have a coffee with me, Alice? I always go into the café about this time."

Suzanne closed her paint box and rose to go, leaving her easel and brushes where they lay, anchored against the wind by two giant stones. I started to remonstrate, but then remembered that this was hardly a city like

New York, or Paris for that matter. It was a safe bet there were no easel thieves in Ste. Ruffin.

"Don't tell me that you are a worrier," my new friend said teasingly. "I thought movie stars do not worry about anything."

"I'm no movie star," I confessed. "Can't you tell?"

Suzanne walked me past the boutique where, she assured me, I'd be able to find any of a dozen little items a woman always found herself without, no matter how carefully she's packed for a trip. She pointed out a couple of cafés close to the water, but they were shut for the winter.

I absolutely loved the one we wound up in, back in the town square. We went in about eleven-thirty and I didn't leave until close to three. It wasn't the food or the coffee or the young red wine that kept me there, as good as they all were; it was Suzanne herself. We really hit it off, and ended up telling each other our life story—with all due embellishments or omissions.

I left with the promise that I would return to the wharf as soon as my schedule permitted. Then I headed toward the inn, taking the slightly different, more roundabout route that Suzanne had recommended, so that I might see the resident potter's studio.

I passed the trailers that housed the French technicians on the film crew, who had been in Ste. Ruffin at least a week before the American contingent arrived.

There was a ragtag, drunken soccer game in progress and I made a wide detour. But not before I spotted Ray Allen Penze among the revelers. He was swearing and clowning outrageously, as drunk as any of the others.

I was more than a little put out by his behavior. What a strange way to mourn the death of his lover and patron a bare twenty-four hours after her demise.

Then I got angry. Because what he should have been doing was consoling Dorothy's cats, who must have been frightened and missing all her doting attention.

Just as I was entering my cottage I got really angry—I noticed that the door to Ray Allen's quarters was ajar. Didn't that fool know that you can't leave a door open that way and expect to find three cats there when you decide to saunter back in?

I walked quickly over to his cottage, took hold of the doorknob, and was about to pull the door shut when I realized someone was inside.

I knocked lightly. There was no answer. I walked in.

A young woman was standing in the center of the large room, her back to the door. She was holding one of the cats in her arms and swaying with it as though rocking a baby.

Then she sensed my presence. She turned and greeted me warmly, as if we were old friends.

But I didn't know this girl . . . did I?

I couldn't respond to her greeting, anyway,

because I found myself tongue-tied, mesmerized by her long golden hair.

It was the same kind of hair I had had once, as a child. A brilliant white-gold waterfall tumbling down my back.

My eyes filled with tears as I stared at her; not for the corruption of time, but for my grandmother. How she had loved to brush my golden hair. She used to tell me that with hair like that I was sure to be rescued by a daring knight if ever I was held captive in a castle by an evil dragon or sorcerer. All I had to do was let my hair down, and the brave knight would climb up my hair and save me and we would live happily ever after.

Being of a practical bent, I asked my grandmother how a young damsel in distress would have the neck muscles to support an armored knight using her hair as a ladder. Gram was aghast at such an unromantic question.

The young woman with the golden hair flashed another beautiful smile at me. And then I noticed the pair of dark-tinted spectacles in the pocket of her camp shirt. Then I knew.

It was Alison Chevigny.

"I'm sorry," I said. "I didn't recognize you with your hair . . . without your glasses."

"I wanted to make sure they'd been fed," she said by way of explanation. Then she added almost sheepishly, "I knew they would be lonely, too. I don't think Mr. Penze really puts himself out over them."

"Agreed," I said acidly.

We chatted a few minutes about Penze's feline problems; then she left.

Six almond eyes watched me as I sat down on the bed. I was very relieved that all the cats seemed to be doing well. They were beautiful Abyssinians—affectionate enough, but completely self-possessed. Three long-legged, ruddy browns ticked with black. Like miniature cougars, some say. Like Egyptian tomb cats, others say.

Then the cat that Alison had been cradling jumped up on the bed beside me.

"Hello, you. Do you want to play?"

She looked as if she did. I pulled her left front leg gently.

The cat yawned.

I let out a startled laugh. She was adorable. I pulled the leg again.

The cat yawned again. How odd. "Sleepy?" I asked, stroking her back. No response.

I gave the same leg another gentle tug. A yawn followed, right on cue.

This encounter was becoming more and more delightful.

I decided to pull the cat's *right* front leg.

She rolled over. A second pull elicited the same acrobatic response.

I went back to the left leg. Yawn.

Right leg . . . roll over.

Left leg . . . yawn.

I got off the bed then and took a long look at the lovely golden cat, as if I were seeing her for the first time.

I realized I hadn't been playing with just any old Abby.

I had been playing with the most famous cat in America . . . the star of the ubiquitous television commercials for the men's cologne Your Night at Maud's (Ta Nuit Chez Maud). In the ads, the cat continues to yawn as a parade of vacuously handsome men wearing the wrong scent try to woo her owner. But when the last debonair Euro-type appears wearing Your Night at Maud's, the cat rolls over in ecstasy.

The feline in those ads, called Maud, had even eclipsed the fame of Morris, the 9-Lives cat. Department stores carried Maud dolls; there were Maud calendars; a line of Maud clothing . . . the works.

I was looking at a superstar—even if I couldn't ask for her autograph.

"I can't believe it's you, Maud! What on earth are you doing here?" was all I could think to say for the moment. Then I added, "And who are these other two beauties . . . your stunt doubles?"

Maud looked blankly at me over her shoulder and took up with a little red rubber ball. I let myself out silently, making sure the door was shut.

Once outside, a very simple thought came to me. This movie, this trip, the whole cinematic adventure in France, was probably financed by Maud. Dorothy Dodd must have made millions from the yawning Abyssinian. But why hadn't I known that Dorothy owned the famous cat? Why hadn't I ever heard about them as a team? It seemed most odd. But then I remembered that show biz animals are all incorporated because they get residuals and the names of the corporations were even more ludicrous than the names of film production companies—like Little Miss Horner Farm. And I remembered that no one knew who really owned Lassie until the day that gentleman died and his obituary in the papers identified him as the owner of the histrionic collie.

I hurried back to my cottage to tell Bushy and Pancho who their next-door neighbor was.

4

When I stepped out of my room the next morning I was wearing one of the outfits I had purchased during my New York shopping fever. This number was very short and high-bodiced, with balloon sleeves—a kind of meditation on a peasant dress. Believe me, I knew it was an altogether inappropriate dress for a statuesque, forty-one-year-old woman. Not to mention its inappropriate price tag. But it wouldn't be honest to say I don't know what possessed me to buy it, because I do know. I had once seen a photo of Brigitte Bardot wearing such a dress at the Cannes Film Festival. And since she had once been my ideal of a movie actress . . . and since I was going to make a movie in France . . . and since I'm so bad with money . . . well, you can see where the delusion lay.

But the dress was inappropriate for still another reason: it was insanely cold that morning. The cutting wind gave the lie to the placid blue morning sky. I turned back immediately and found my sweater coat.

As I made my way toward the dining room the sun appeared again, just for a few seconds, and then vanished. This was a weird morning indeed. I could almost feel the weather on me, unfriendly, menacing.

Also, for the first time I noticed the reddish hue of the Camargue winter plant life, a unique phenomenon that, according to my guidebook, has something to do with the high salt content of the soil. For some reason that hue frightened me.

I found that I was shivering even in the thick sweater. I went back to my cottage once more and put on the Navy pea coat Basillio had pressed on me the night before I left New York. I don't think it's ever taken me so long to get to my morning cup of coffee.

There were more staff than guests in the dining room. The ratio seemed to run about four to one. I tried out my fractured French on the short, stocky young waitress. *"Bonjour,"* I said. *"C'est froid."*

She smiled indulgently. *"Non, madame. C'est normale."* And she handed me a large cup of coffee.

As I shed my coat and sweater I wondered if she recognized the Bardot dress. True, she might not even be old enough to remember Bardot the actress, but surely the young people knew her as an animal rights pioneer. That was another reason I was convinced BB was the archetypal movie star—the way her people had taken her to their hearts. She was an institution. For a movie star, acting ability should always be a secondary consideration.

I was all alone in the room now. I couldn't tell what kind of jam was in the little pot next to my plate, but I dug in anyway and spread it thickly on my croissant. Delicious! Superb! So was the coffee, but that was no surprise. I maintain that the French make the best coffee in the world. But as a few of my friends point out, I haven't seen that much of the world. Tony Basillio, for instance, merely laughs at my assertion. The French know nothing about coffee compared to the Italians, he says. They don't even stand up to a comparison with the Turks, to hear him tell it.

Just as I was taking my last bit of the excellent little baguette, holding it lovingly in my hand, in popped Cilla Hood, who seemed to be perpetually out of breath.

"Everybody stay right where you are, please," Cilla called, then looked around and realized that I *was* everybody. "Oh," she said. "I'll go find the others. Just don't leave—okay, Alice?"

I didn't answer right away. I just held eye contact with her as she backed out of the room.

"Cilla!" I spoke not angrily but firmly enough to halt her jerky movements. "What are you trying to say?"

"He's back!" she yelled, then disappeared through the arched entryway.

He? Who? Oh, of course. Brian Watts. Our producer. Early morning mystery call. American Consulate. Marseilles. We're in France now. Wake up, Alice.

I took another croissant.

Alison Chevigny came in then, hair pulled back into a ponytail, wearing her signature dark glasses. She nodded wanly in my direction and sat at the next table, Ray Allen Penze close on her heels.

I shot a dirty look over at him, as if warning him that he had to make sure his cottage door was shut and he had to take proper care of the great Maud, along with her sisters, unless he wanted strychnine in his champagne, or whatever it was he drank when he played soccer. He didn't seem to mind my look at all. But that was because he never saw it. He was focused on Alison, who was beginning to look more and more like the young Catherine Deneuve to me.

Five minutes later Monsieur Braque arrived, still dopey, I guessed, from sleep. Surprising me, he smiled civilly at me and sat at my table.

Brian and Cilla came in next. And I had been chagrined at *my* less than appropriate outfit! I saw that Brian was wearing what was easily a $500 running suit, zipped all the way up to his neck, as if he were an Olympic hopeful rather than an overweight, middle-aged film producer. But any urge on my part to laugh out loud was soon suppressed. I looked at his face and instantly saw the worry and pain written there.

Brian did not sit down. He said levelly, meeting each of our eyes in turn, "I am afraid I have some distressing news . . . as if we haven't already had enough of it."

He gestured harshly to Cilla, who had not yet left his side, and she took a seat.

"It seems that Dorothy," Brian continued, "left very clear instructions with her attorney." He removed a slip of paper from his pocket and read from it in overenunciated tones: "'Upon my death all funding of the film project presently titled *The Emptying* shall cease immediately and not be reinstated under any conditions."

I felt as if someone were standing on my stomach.

Nobody spoke, nobody asked for details, but we all knew what it meant. It meant the film was dead. Dead in the water. Even before it had begun.

Brian held up his hand. "I don't want anyone to panic. I don't want you to despair. Yes, it looks bad. No doubt about it. But, as the Americans say, it isn't over till it's over. Now, believe me, I have a few tricks up my sleeve. Just give me a little more time. And most important—I want everyone to stay put . . . right where we are.

"The inn was paid for in advance, so your accommodations are all taken care of.

"We're going to have to let the technicians

go, of course. But if the project can be saved we can get them back on pretty short notice."

He halted, nervously moving the zipper of his suit up and down on its track. "Just remember—we're not dead yet."

I heard him repeat that phrase—we're not dead yet—as, one by one, we filed out of the wake.

Once in my cottage I fell wearily onto my bed.

"Well, dear friend," I said to Bushy when he joined me, "I guess we won't be going to Paris, after all. You won't get to see a Paris rat and I won't be a movie star. Whose disappointment will be greater, Bushman? Whose credit card will die first?"

He seemed to understand the extent of the tragedy, because he pressed his nose against my forehead and kept it there for a long while. It was futile to tell Pancho, I realized, who had never been very keen on the idea of me on the silver screen.

My intense self-pity lasted about twenty minutes. And then my good sense kicked in. Something was going on around us that dwarfed in importance whether or not an arty thriller would see the light of day.

I realized that if Dorothy had left those instructions with her lawyer, she must have had some sort of premonition of her own death.

I got off the bed, and after a few minutes pacing sat down in the old rocking chair positioned between the cottage's two front windows.

Yes, indeed. Those instructions were a vindictive sort of act—a payback—as though she had felt that someone involved with the movie would or could be the cause of her death.

In other words, Dorothy must have believed that there was a chance she might be murdered.

Was the accident just a mask for murder?

It was an outlandish idea. I started to rock in my chair. Hadn't we all seen the accident occur? Yes. But all we had seen was *what* happened . . . not *why* or *how* it had happened.

I slowed my rocking. Another question began forming in my mind—a damned important question. Why would anyone connected with this film want to murder his or her benefactor? It made no sense.

Unless . . . unless . . .

Pancho flew by me and dived under the bed.

. . . Maud! A person might easily murder for possession of that multimillion-dollar cat.

Was that it? Ray Allen Penze wanted Maud? He was tired of being a filmic gigolo. He wanted his own milk cow—a Madison Avenue invention named Maud.

Whoa, Alice, whoa. I realized my logic was beginning to escape the bounds of reality. After all, Penze had been unbelievably cavalier in his treatment of the Abyssinians after Dorothy's death. He had paid no attention to them at all. He couldn't even be bothered to make sure the door to the cottage was closed. In fact, maybe he didn't even know that one of those cats was the superstar Maud. A shrewd woman like Dorothy Dodd might not have disclosed to her pretty boy protégé that one of her cats was a gold mine.

I leaned forward on the chair and looked out at each of the other cottages. Who else would know about Maud? Anyone or no one. I had no idea.

Oh, my. All these speculations had begun to weary me, exciting as they were. After all, my screen career had just been brutally crushed. It was not a good mixture.

Maybe a long walk would help clear my head. I decided to go into Ste. Ruffin and see Suzanne Aubert.

I got into my warmest clothes and went down the path, through the village, and onto the freezing wharf. But she was not there painting. The wharf was deserted. I remembered the café and walked there quickly. I had the sense that it would not just be pleasant to see my new friend . . . but that it was necessary—vital—for my own peace of mind and health.

She was sitting at the same table that she and I had taken the other day. Her easel was propped up against the back wall like a wet umbrella. She waved to me and I joined her. The old couple who ran the café also greeted me warmly. I relaxed at once.

It was such a welcoming place. Ancient and yet spotless. The old chairs and tables were dull with age. The whitewashed walls were hung here and there with paintings of the Camargue sand dunes and the high-steepled church in the square. A lovable, floppy-eared dog named Boyer visited each table in five-minute relays, laying his head on one's lap and expecting to be liberally scratched for his efforts. There was a breakfront along one wall groaning with bottles and jugs and pungent cheeses under glass bells. A low swinging door connected the café to the small kitchen where the food was prepared.

It was very early in the day—and against my better judgment—but I ordered a glass of wine. I sipped it and watched, as did Suzanne, while Boyer inspected her painting supplies.

"If he raises his leg on my easel I will hit him with a chair," Suzanne said.

But Boyer was respectful. He sniffed a few moments longer and then wandered off under a table. His shaggy face had become completely mournful. So mournful that I all but burst into tears looking at him.

Suzanne was all concern. "Alice, something is wrong, yes? What is the matter?"

"It's the damn movie," I blurted out. "There isn't going to be one. They're shutting down."

"But why?"

I waited until I had squeezed back my ridiculous tears to tell her in brief, realizing I should not have wine in the morning.

"It did not sound like a good film," she said with dismissive Gallic reasoning.

I laughed. Then she laughed, too. Then Boyer came over to investigate the commotion and lay his head in my lap. I obliged him with a few pats and scratches.

The high-pitched sounds of a car braking suddenly shattered the café calm.

Seconds later a young black woman swung in through the door. She looked around rather imperiously, spotted the old proprietor, and strode over to him, the tap-tap of her dazzling red high-heeled boots echoing through the room.

Her coloring was a very pretty beige, and her hair was cut very short, in the Jean Seberg tradition. And like Seberg, this young woman had clear, creamy skin and was of small build, thin and wiry and seeming to vibrate with health and energy.

I could hear random words of her conversation with the old monsieur: "Can you direct me?" and "the film company."

So she was a fellow American.

The proprietors exchanged words with each other and then began to answer the young woman's questions in halting English. She listened attentively, then turned to go.

Then she saw me. I was sure I'd been discreet and hadn't been obvious about eavesdropping on her exchange with the owners. Nonetheless, she stood there staring at me for a long moment, and then walked halfway toward our table and addressed me directly.

"Aren't you Alice Nestleton?"

For heaven's sake—this was like having someone come up to you in Saudi Arabia and tell you they loved you in that high school production of *Glass Menagerie*.

"You are, aren't you?"

"Yes."

She nodded, traversed the remaining distance, and boldly pulled a chair up to our table, an implied "May I?" in her body language.

"You don't remember me," she stated.

"I'm afraid I don't."

"Of course you don't. And for just this *one time*, mind you, I'm going to forgive you. But I won't be so nice if you cut me dead at any important restaurants back in the States."

Suzanne and I laughed, though neither of us quite understood. "I can't believe we've met and I don't remember you," I said.

"Well," she said nonchalantly, "it has been a few years. Think party. Think Gramercy Park mansion tasteful within an inch of its life. Think late autumn and a lot of bittersweet conversations about integrity and the business. Lots and lots of theater people. A few movie people with high school diplomas. The hosts were very lovely heroin addicts. They've pretended she still has a career for so long that she's actually working again."

No, I *couldn't* believe we'd met and I didn't remember her. Of course, it was difficult to tell whether she was being serious.

"And," she continued, "we even met once before that. But of course nobody could be expected to remember me from then. I was nothing more than the bulemic, token black girl reporter for the high school drama review. There was a benefit in the old Chelsea Mews Theatre . . . I forget who was to benefit . . . and you recited some well-executed if shamelessly self-indulgent lines by a woman poet I'd never heard of before—and haven't again to this day."

"I remember the benefit vaguely," I said, a bit sheepish.

"My name is Mona Columbia. What's the wine like here?"

"The film critic?"

"In the chilled and all too mortal flesh," she said. She shook my hand and that of Suzanne Aubert. Then she held up two fingers of her tiny hand and signaled for service.

Yes, I had surely heard of Mona Columbia. She was a quick-witted, very aggressive critic who had alienated so many American film luminaries that the French had taken her to their bosom. She soon abandoned the States to become a world-class writer-commentator. At least that was what I had heard. Most of her pieces were over my head, as far as "the cinema" was concerned. She tended to bring in the most arcane and erudite elements of the history of film and auteur theory when she wrote—as well as anything else she felt necessary to discuss—most of it equally arcane.

"I've been pretending to be Jack Kerouac the last few weeks . . . you know, on the road," Mona laughed and drank a bit of her wine. "But actually I think Orwell is more me . . . down and

out in Provence . . . no, that doesn't scan, does
it? Well, you sort of know what I mean, yes?"

She spoke so quickly and intensely that one
found oneself leaning in toward her words, so
as not to miss something.

" . . . and now I'm just plain tired. Damn
lucky I met you here, you being one of the
stars of *The Emptying*. No offense, Alice, but
the word on the street is that Antonioni
sketched out this script on the back of a nap-
kin in '78, thought better of it, and wiped the
marinara off his lips with it."

Mona threw back her head and laughed.

"Oh, God, pay no attention to me. I'm only
teasing. Listen, VF is paying me good money to
do this piece on Brian Watts and his movie. I
know he's a pompous ass . . . they know
it . . . you must know it, too—"

"VF?" I interrupted. "What is VF?"

"*Vanity Fair*, Alice," said Suzanne, almost
impatient with me.

"Anyway," Mona went on, "one does have to
live. Business is business. I need the money.
Brian and the rest of you guys need the pub-
licity. And they'll edit all the life out of my
piece anyway. So everybody'll be happy. Besides, I kind of like Brian. Don't you . . . kind
of?"

Suzanne could not take her eyes off Mona.

I still did not recall meeting her at those
places she'd mentioned, especially the glamorous party in Gramercy Park, but my social
memory was always bad. But that didn't mat-

ter now. Mona Columbia had to be brought up-to-date.

"There're some things you'll want to know about, Mona," I said. "Dorothy Dodd was killed in an automobile accident on her way to Ste. Ruffin."

She stiffened. "What?"

"She was driving into town. There was a wreck. She was killed instantly."

"Oh, Lord . . . How terrible."

"Also," I continued, "some instructions she left with her attorneys have come to light. The long and short of it is that all funding for the movie terminates when she . . . terminates."

Mona thrust her hyperactive little hands into the pockets of her exquisitely tailored riding jacket as if she couldn't trust what they might do next. She repeated, "Terrible. Terrible." Then she ordered another glass of wine. I took up my glass again as well. After a while the drooling dog, Boyer, loped over for a few strokes from any takers. Suzanne shooed him away when she saw Mona recoil.

"I never understood the fascination with dogs," she said, one hand clutching at the top of her white turtleneck. "Especially big ones. I mean, they're just so terribly . . . oppressive in their devotion."

"That is seldom a problem with cats," I said.

"Good. Oh, that's right . . . Aren't you someone who lives with twenty or thirty of them? Like Sandy Dennis."

"Not quite that many. But how could you

possibly remember that about me? From one
meeting at a party."

"Memory," she said, tapping her forehead.
"My curse. And I mean *really* my curse. Because it's so quirky and selective. Do I remember the capital of Iowa? No. Can I tell you off
the top of my head when the first American
slave was manumitted? No. But ask me for
Walter Huston's Broadway credits—or what
filter Haskell Wexler used in a particular shot
in *Medium Cool*. I can tell you those things. Of
course, I'm hoping you won't ask me either of
those things just at *this* moment."

We sat drinking for a while longer. The sunlight came through the café in elliptical waves.
Mona asked me what I would do if the picture
deal really fell through. I said I didn't know.

Then she said, "You know, we also have a
mutual friend in New York."

"Who is that?"

"Chu Chu Bailyn."

I turned the name over in my mind. "Do you
mean Agatha Bailyn?"

"*Is* that her name? I never knew. But anyway, she maintains you're the best actor in
New York City."

I laughed, a little embarrassed. Agatha Bailyn
and I had been in a lunatic production of *Trojan
Women* in the late 1970s. Then she began to do
performance art, becoming known, apparently, as
Chu Chu, and mounted a lewd one-woman attack
against everything. She was billed as a feminist,
but it was really total nihilism. It was a media
event every time she performed—pickets and cops

and TV cameras and hate groups and supporters. She was a smart woman, a very good actor, and I hadn't heard from her in years.

"What is she doing now?" I asked Mona.

"She still lives in New York. But mostly she works in Germany. She's a big cabaret star in Berlin. Decadent, isn't it? They love her over there. Their appetite for American avant-gardists simply cannot be sated, it seems. But why not? It all seems harmless enough. And . . . oh, she's making a documentary on Turkish women workers in Germany."

"I'll look for it. Please give her my best when you see her."

To an observer, I'm sure we looked like a group of friends just catching up with one another's lives. It must have looked as if we were completely comfortable together—that we were getting along famously. And I guess we were. But the truth of it was that we were really a very odd trio—Mona, Suzanne, and I.

Mona began a monologue detailing her meandering trip through the French countryside. It was a fascinating narrative—everything a good story should be: funny, suspenseful, filled with wonderful details and insights. She had that kind of penetrating wit that made her more likable the more she spoke. And she had the terrific ability to take a simple event and expand it into a cosmic continuum of leaps that the listener didn't have to fully understand to fully enjoy. She told us, for instance, about a pretty young farm woman she saw walking along the road, and managed to tie it seamlessly into seven or eight films—perhaps one of which I'd even heard of—made in the late forties about the French Resistance. Ultimately, she even brought the story around to the iconographic significance of Joan of Arc . . . and then, somewhere during the deconstruction of Carl Dreyer's oeuvre, she lost me utterly. Mona was quite a talker.

And the more she talked, the closer I felt to Suzanne. And, I had the unshakable sense that, in some way, there was a fourth woman there at the table with us: Dorothy Dodd. And maybe Maud, too.

Draining her second glass of wine, Mona turned to me, sighed, and said rather wearily, "Well, I suppose it's about time for you to take me to your leader. If you'd be so kind."

"That would be Brian?" I said.

"None other."

Mona said her gracious and very charming good-byes to Suzanne, taking another ten minutes to apologize, in her way, for having talked so much. Suzanne said she hadn't minded a bit. And I'm sure she wasn't lying.

Mona and I walked out to her dust-coated car—a vintage red T4 Triumph, low and lean and very James Dean, the top rolled down in spite of the weather. I hadn't seen a car like it in years. She retrieved her own dark glasses from the glove compartment and then offered me her spare pair. Immediately, I thought of our PA, Alison Chevigny, and her ubiquitous dark glasses.

I don't know when it was that young women

developed such a fanatical attachment to dark glasses—or why. I often wonder what expensive shades symbolize to them, for surely they must symbolize something. I remember searching my mind as we drove, trying to visualize Bardot in dark glasses. I couldn't. And I declined Mona's kind offer.

She drove very much like she talked—all over the place. Sort of wild. Sort of unstoppable. I pointed out the encampment of trailers that the technicians were already beginning to abandon.

A few minutes later we were pulling into the parking lot of the inn. The death vehicle was still in place. Mona slowed for just a moment when she drove past it, and she turned her head briefly to look at the shattered windshield.

I looked at my watch. "La-di-da. Cocktail time again. Where do the days go?"

Mona looked at me quizzically.

"More than likely they're all in there," I said, nodding toward the main building. "There isn't much to do now but wait for the news—one way or the other."

Brian was so happy to see Mona I almost expected him to pick her up in his arms. Guiding her around the room to introduce her to everyone, he described her as one of the world's great film critics, and one of the very few who "understood" what he was trying to do in the business. She looked suitably chagrined by it all, but remained polite.

It was obvious that everyone in that room had been drinking for some time. The wine I had ordered at the café was still very much with me. I sat down quietly at one of the small tables and had a few salted nuts with my fizzy water.

I resolved to watch the proceedings from the sidelines. I needed to get back into my rocking chair logic mode . . . to think about the strange death and stranger vengeance of Dorothy Dodd . . . but there was too much noise and color and desperate mirth going on. To think clearly, I would have to leave. And I didn't want to do that just yet.

Brian had maneuvered Mona into a more isolated part of the room and, drink in hand, was pontificating. Mona had, in fact, removed a notepad from her jacket pocket and was list-lessly jotting down a few words from time to time. No doubt, the brilliant young woman would be able to get just as good a story out of the film's not being made as the one she might have written on the making of it.

Cilla Hood joined them then, refilling Brian's glass and finishing his sentence at the same time. She filled in the gaps whenever his memory failed him and generally acted as his one-woman cheerleading squad.

In the middle of one of Brian's stories, Mona raised her hand to signal a time-out. She took leave of him, promising to return shortly. I saw her walk toward the bar. Maybe to get another drink, maybe simply to give her eardrums a rest. In the end, she did not order

a drink. She stood massaging her eyes for a
few moments, and then started back toward
Brian and Cilla.

On her way across the room, she did something very peculiar. She passed Claude
Braque's chair, and as she did so, never
breaking stride, I swear her hand brushed deliberately over the back of his neck. The inti-
macy of the gesture was almost palpable.

When she was well past him, Braque turned
to stare after her. The look on his face was one
of wrenching anguish.

I had seen variants on that look before—but
nothing that matched the purity of it. Not on
my ex-husband's face as he waxed poetic
about my being an erotic treasure whose loss
he would never get over. Nor on Basillio's face
at the end of a lovely evening when I leave him
in the taxi. Sometimes those looks make me
laugh. Not this time.

But no one else seemed to have picked up
on the arcane little drama played by Mona
and Claude. And indeed, during Mona's long
visit in the café earlier, she hadn't mentioned
a word about Claude. Were they secret lovers?
Why secret? It was clear that these two people
knew each other.

I ordered another bottle of water. For the
first time since I sat down I was surveying the
scene like the old Alice Nestleton, the criminal
investigator, the snoop. Not Alice Nestleton,
the actress, who almost became rich and famous.

Or was I looking at the scene so analytically,

so minutely, because I now considered myself cat-sitter to the greatest star of all—Maud.

Brian had started to emote again for Mona. Was he telling her about his plan to pull the chestnuts out of the fire? Did he have one?

Mona still had her notepad in hand, but she was no longer taking notes. A fascinating young woman. Why couldn't I remember meeting her in New York? She wasn't the kind of person you forgot. I had no doubt that she was telling the truth, but . . . but . . .

Something else was beginning to bother me about Mona Columbia. I remembered that from the first moment she walked into the café in the village she had spoken only English. Even to the French proprietors of whom she had initially asked directions.

Why? Why hadn't she spoken French? She had been in Europe for several years on and off. In fact, I understood that she wrote many of her articles in French, maybe German as well. Why speak English when she didn't have to? Was it a kind of cultural nationalism? Doubtful, since Mona was trying to be a transnational Renaissance woman.

I asked for another dish of nuts and turned my attention to Ray Allen Penze. He was dressed preposterously, in what may have been all the rage—I didn't know. But he seemed to be doing an imitation of a rap singer, replete with hooded sweatshirt and baseball cap worn backward.

He was standing over a seated Alison Chevigny, who was staring straight ahead through another pair of dark glasses. There was a very pretty rhinestone comb holding back the tumble of her hair. She was drinking what I guessed to be a Campari and soda.

Ray Allen appeared to be laying it on pretty thick—posturing, throwing around references to Anjelica and the risotto at Spago. He was determined to be perceived as hip, desirable, knowing. Well, he *was* good-looking; it was his one asset he hadn't overestimated.

Alison, however, was not rising to the bait. She sat there calmly, listening mostly, occasionally making a brief comment. Of course, I couldn't see her eyes. And it is hard to make judgments about people when you can't see their eyes. There was a popular song I dimly recalled—you can't hide your lying eyes.

In time, Alison became less distracted. At least she was looking directly at Ray Allen, and not shrinking from his occasional touch. He had taken a chair and pulled it up close to hers. I sensed from his posture, from the way he leaned in fluidly toward her, that he was now being terribly "sincere."

It appeared that another potential romance was taking shape. My my. Dead time on a movie set must mean a veritable explosion of coupling.

Suddenly I felt one of those washes of loneliness that can just roll over one. I found myself wishing that Basillio were here. He'd have something salty to say about Ray Allen Penze, I knew. I was missing Basillio a lot. Or maybe I was just getting homesick.

"I am so touched! So veddy veddy touched that you're giving me this surprise party. But it is emphatically not my birthday!" Someone was doing a very good impression of Peter O'Toole.

We all turned toward the speaker. It was Sidney Rice—with scarf and cane. What a marvelous entrance!

Brian rushed over to meet him. We all followed.

Sidney looked a great deal like the character who'd made him famous—he'd received the Oscar for best supporting actor—so many years ago: the tubercular physician at a Japanese prison camp in Singapore, who sacrifices his life for those in his care. Reed-thin, but so handsome in that pale upper-crust British way. Able to overcome physical weakness through nobility of spirit.

"They were going to release me tomorrow morning," he explained, "but I just walked out and hitched a ride. It isn't that I missed you lot. In all honesty, I just needed a drink."

Alison brought him a large brandy.

Gradually the greeters dropped away and Sidney stood there as alone as when he entered, cane and brandy in the same hand.

"Do you mind?" he asked, pulling out the empty chair across from me with some difficulty.

"My pleasure," I said, and with my foot reached under the table and helped him out by pushing against the chair leg.

He sat down heavily.

"How are you feeling, Sidney?"

"Like Quasimodo after he first spots Maureen O'Hara."

"You mean excited?"

"No. Impotent." He drank his brandy slowly. He looked in pain. He looked his age; the furrows on his handsome face were like deep cuts in a piece of fruit. The British agent in the movie, his role, required someone about forty-five. Sidney would need a lot of help from makeup.

"Aren't you drinking?" he asked me.

"I already have."

"Well, even if you don't drink, it's nice sitting here with you. Not only are you good-looking, you're the first American actress I've met in a long time who doesn't hate me."

"What do you do to them?"

"Not a thing. It's being British. All American actors seem to hate the English. You know that."

"For a time maybe. But that was because ninety percent of all the shows on Broadway had British casts."

"Not our bloody fault if American audiences like imported shows."

"Audiences like what they're told to like."

"Aha! Another little fascist of the footlights."

"But then again, a lot of mothers told a lot of children to like spinach, and that didn't work. The fact is, British performers tend to be likable. The way they speak. The way they carry themselves. The way they're trained."

"Well, thank you so much, Alice. Would you

like to hear a joke about how wonderful we British performers are?"

"Very well."

"It goes something like this: A very famous Brit actor with a great profile and a weakness for drink picks up a woman in a cheap bar. They spend the night in his hotel room and the next morning, after she's dressed, she says, 'Well, I'll be going now, Mr. Pilkington. How about twenty-five dollars?' And he turns to her and says, 'Oh, thank you, my dear. It would come in quite handy.'"

I might have heard that story before; I couldn't remember. I didn't find it at all funny, but laughed to be polite.

"You know, Sidney, I first studied acting at the Guthrie in Minneapolis and they copied a lot of your Royal Academy programs. We even had to take courses in fencing and dance. But then, when I came to New York, I studied with Method teachers, who positively loathed English technique."

"I can just imagine you fencing," he said.

"Don't be so quick to laugh. I was very good. Though I really hated wearing that mask."

Sidney rested his hands on top of his cane and then placed his chin on his hands. He looked as if he might do an impression of Auden now.

"I suppose it all comes down to the terrible two," he said thoughtfully.

"Two what?"

"If you're going to try and judge the relative merits of British against American actors, it

ultimately comes down to two, because that is
the only way to judge them . . . a pair at a
time."

"And which two do you have in mind?"

"Let's stick with Olivier and Brando."

"A good pair."

"Yes. Now, how does one evaluate them
mano a mano? In my humble opinion, they are
both great actors. But Olivier has the edge."

Life really is strange. I was in the wilds of the
French countryside with a fellow actor—a man
who had distinguished himself in a handful of
quality films and then become a kind of gen-
teel has-been in the industry—who'd nearly
been killed in the auto accident that had taken
the life of our producer. And what do we do?
Get into a typical acting students' drugstore
conversation, like teenagers.

"Yes," I agreed, "Olivier was a great actor.
But Brando could do everything he could do—
and then more. He could do roles that Olivier
simply could not."

"Such as?"

"Stanley Kowalski, of course."

"Olivier could do Kowalski. He just
wouldn't."

It was the kind of comment that was guar-
anteed to irritate me, and my face must have
shown it, because Sidney reached across and
patted my hand in a fatherly way. "I think perhaps we should discuss the merits of French
hospitals rather than actors on one side of the
ocean or the other."

I shrugged my shoulders.

"The place they had me," he said, "was laughingly called Nom de Dieu. Reminded me of the one in Hemingway's *A Farewell to Arms* . . . except I didn't get laid."

I smiled appreciatively, but then said, "We could talk about the accident and what you saw and heard just before the crash."

His eyes widened. "Why in God's name would you want to know about that?"

"Curiosity, I suppose."

He didn't speak for a few moments. He seemed to be deciding whether to say anything at all. "I am afraid there isn't much to tell . . . nothing to appease your 'curiosity,' . . . no near death experience or anything remotely like it. All I remember is that we came to a sharp curve and I set my body for the braking—the way you do in a car, as though the pedal were under your own foot. But instead of braking, slowing down to turn, the car just seemed to . . . accelerate . . . straight ahead. That's all. It was over with very quickly."

"Were there any arguments during the drive?"

"Arguments? No. Everyone was having a high old time. She—Dorothy—was joshing Claude about his reputation as a ladies' man. And then she began to rib me. Told me that the inn had been forewarned about my drinking and had laid in all my favorite brands. It was half the budget of the film, she said. Things like that."

He drained the remaining brandy from his

glass and looked around the room in a kind of desperation.

"Are you all right?" I asked.

"Yes, yes," he answered. Sidney looked up gratefully at the waitress who had appeared with the brandy bottle.

"You know," he said after a minute, more relaxed now, "I'd heard a lot of things about Dorothy. That she was hard as nails, ruthless, a bitch, and so on. But I found her to be a perfect lady. If a bit nutty. She was perfectly nice to me. Just . . . oh, I don't know . . . "

He turned his attention back to his drink. What did he mean by calling Dorothy nutty? I wondered. What was he trying to tell me? I decided not to press him for now, to let him explain in his own good time.

I found myself examining his ravaged face with interest, admiring his steel-blue eyes. Sidney Rice was, I realized with some discomfort, one of the few older men I have ever been drawn to. I broke my gaze and sat back. I must have been feeling even lonelier and more excluded than I realized.

"It's funny you should ask about the accident, Alice," he finally resumed. "There were a few strange things that happened . . . before."

I waited, my body becoming cramped, anticipatory.

"For one, the ride was the jerkiest I've ever known. Dorothy kept slowing down and then racing ahead."

"Was it the road?"

"No. I'm sure of that. There was no reason

whatever. She'd just slow down to a snail's pace, and then suddenly speed up again. She was like a child in a kiddie car. When Ray Allen said something about it, she behaved as though she had no idea what he was talking about."

"That *is* odd. Anything else?"

"Well . . . yes. At one point, she turned on the windshield wipers. Again, for no reason. Just turned them on. They were wiping up a storm—at absolutely nothing. I was the one who spoke up that time. I asked why she'd turned them on. And she said, as though I were the biggest fool who ever lived, 'I have to get that mud off the windows, don't I? It's hell driving in a rainstorm like this.'

"Then, when someone pointed out that there was no rainstorm, she just laughed. Laughed. I thought she must be having some sort of private joke. I just let it drop. She went back to the slow down and speed up routine, and then . . . a few minutes later . . . Well, you know the end of the story."

Out of nowhere, a hand appeared and grasped his now-empty brandy snifter. Instinctively, Sidney reached out to protect the glass, then smiled when he saw that a fresh drink was replacing the empty glass.

It wasn't the waitress, but Alison, who had performed the honors. She smiled at Sidney and me as she sat down near us. Almost at the same moment I stood up. For some reason the young woman made me very uncomfortable. Perhaps it was the way she had just suddenly appeared. I wasn't sure. But I moved away quickly, leaving the two of them there, and headed over to one of the windows, where a pensive Mona Columbia was standing.

She was alone for the first time since I had brought her to the inn.

"Have you discovered the secret yet?" I asked her.

"What secret?"

"Brian Watts's secret source for the money to make this godforsaken film."

"Oh, that. Sorry, I don't know what's happening on that score. Brian's got an inexhaustible repertoire of double talk. His belief that the film will go ahead may be anchored in reality. And then again, it may not be. But if I were you I wouldn't invest in my wardrobe for the Cannes Festival just yet."

Mona and I both stared out the window for a few minutes, not talking. After listening to her bright, runaway conversation all day, I was trying to imagine what her sudden tumble into silence meant.

"I guess it could get pretty depressing for you here now," she said a minute later.

"That's a pretty good guess."

"Nothing so sad as a group of film people with nothing to film. It brings out the pathetic in everyone."

I laughed gently. "Luckily I'm from the theater . . . when I'm working, that is."

I noticed then that Alison Chevigny had left Sidney alone at his table and was moving toward Mona and me. Damn! Once again, I had that urgent need to get away. I just didn't want to talk to her.

"Mona," I said quickly, "I think I'll say good night now. So long."

And without ever looking back, I walked swiftly out of the room.

On the way to my own quarters I noticed that the curtains on the front window of Ray Allen's cottage were open. I veered off course and went to peek in there. I wanted to see how Maud and the other Abbys were doing.

What a lovely sight. All three were draped over the big bed. Like the three little kittens who'd lost their mittens. My laughter didn't last long. I realized that they were waiting—still—for Dorothy. I looked over at the wrecked van in the lot. And then back again to the cottage. I didn't know which sight was sadder.

As I thought of those darling cats waiting for someone who would never appear, Sidney Rice's words seemed to resound inside my head. The things he remembered—snippets of conversation and Dorothy's bizarre behavior—were all inchoate now. They meant little.

But whether he'd misremembered things or misinterpreted them, too many snippets had accumulated to be ignored. I couldn't ignore them, at any rate. I was anxious about the fate of the movie. Disappointed. Tired. Lonely. Alienated.

I was, however, no fool.

Dorothy Dodd had been murdered. I knew that now.

And the reason for the murder was that

beautiful Abyssinian who was worth more money than I could ever dream of.

I tapped on the windowpane. One of the kitties looked up. I think it was Maud. I waved to her. "They won't get away with it, girlie—don't you worry," I said low. "They can't do this to you—you're a star."

She almost seemed to have heard me. Because she started to roll over. I could see the preliminary move. Then she stopped. Oh, it was enough though.

5

I skipped dinner that evening and stayed alone in my cottage with my cats. It was a difficult evening. I needed someone to trust, someone to speak to, someone to whom I could lay out the contours of what I knew was murder.

I realized full well that both Basillio and Detective Rothwax of RETRO, if they'd been here, would have scoffed at my theory. But each of them, I knew, would have been profoundly troubled by all these little evidentiary innuendos, if I may coin a phrase—a phrase not much more literate, I guess, than "we followed the perpetrator."

The real problem was, I didn't know what to do next.

Who *could* I talk to? Who *did* I trust? Maybe my French friend, Suzanne Aubert. But she was in the village, not here at the inn. She wasn't one of us.

And there was the time factor. How much longer would I be in France? Perhaps as little as forty-eight hours, if Brian Watts was unable to get a promise of funding.

And, nagging at me, always there, was the possibility that I was merely dealing in a paranoid form with my own disenchantment. In other words, my gingerbread dream of fame and riches as a movie star had ended the moment that van crashed into the church wall. Maybe the idea that it was just an accident—that mere chance had made it impossible for me ever to have another wild shopping spree—was just intolerable to me, too much to bear. So I constructed a malevolent entity—a murderer. At least that way there was some justification for what happened, some way to deal with it. And if I found the murderer, at least I'd be salvaging a sliver of triumph from defeat.

Was that what I was doing? I didn't think so. But I knew it was a possibility.

Another long night. I fell asleep just short of midnight and woke just after six A.M.: a farm girl's six hours. That was really all you needed, my grandmother used to say.

Trouble arrived an hour later.

Bushy refused to eat his food. He went off to a corner and began acting very strangely. He sat erect with a funny stare, then lay down flat, then sat up again. He seemed to be in some discomfort.

Then he began to mewl pathetically, and to

prowl the room, taking weird, mincing little steps.

My poor Bushy! Something terrible was happening to him.

I sat on the bed and watched him, uselessly hoping that whatever was ailing him would just go away.

But no such luck. Within half an hour he was wailing grotesquely.

I could wait no longer. I dressed, put him in his carrier, and headed toward the village. Surely Suzanne would know of a veterinarian, or she could help me find one.

But once in the village, I realized that I had no idea where Suzanne lived. And it was too early for her to be at her work on the wharf. I literally leapt in front of an ancient delivery truck that was puttering down the village's main street. The driver stuck his head out the window and cursed me unrestrainedly. I understood not a word, but kept shouting back at him: "Madame Aubert! Suzanne Aubert!" Finally, he understood. He knew exactly where she lived. He mimed the directions to me and I took off.

Suzanne answered the bell immediately. She was in her bathrobe and wearing beautiful fur-lined slippers.

I must have been nearly hysterical, because as soon as she'd taken me inside the house she covered my shoulders with some kind of cloak, as if I were an invalid. Then she asked me why I was wandering around with my cat.

I explained the situation. She told me not to

worry. She said that although there really was no veterinarian in the area, most of the townspeople with animals—certainly most of the herdsmen—depended upon Madame Nair.

"Who is Madame Nair?"

"She is a gypsy woman who lives in the village."

"A what? You mean a—a—*gypsy!*"

"She has a great way with animals, Alice. A gift, really. And actually," Suzanne added, "she is only half gypsy."

I cringed. This was terrible. How could I take poor suffering Bushy to some half-baked fortune-teller? He needed a trained physician, perhaps medicine.

"Is there no real vet in the area?"

"No. You would probably have to go to Arles or Marseilles. And I don't think it will be necessary. Madame Nair is a woman you can trust."

I tapped my fingers nervously on Suzanne's breakfast table. I could hear little whimpers issuing from Bushy's carrier. Time was fleeting. I didn't know what to do. Begin the long drive into one of the neighboring towns? Or consent to visiting this Madame Nair? And where was I going to get a car at this time of morning?

"Tell me, Suzanne, is this woman a herbalist or something?"

"I'm not sure I know what you mean, Alice."

"I mean, does she cure animals with natural things—herbs, berries, spring water, whatever? Does she wander around the marshes picking fronds and slime to use as medicine?"

"I have no idea what Madame Nair does in the marsh," she said, a little confused. "I don't even know if she ever goes there. She is not a young woman."

I had to make a decision quickly. I put my trust in Suzanne.

"Will you take me to this Madame?"

"Of course," she replied. "In a moment." She removed her bathrobe and threw on a long, red-and-white-striped wool winter coat over her blue cotton nightgown. She smiled at me, saying: "When you live near the sea, clothes do not matter." She didn't have to explain her incongruous outfit to me. I liked it. She didn't even change her slippers.

We walked quickly to a narrow, high, ramshackle house not far from the wharf.

A dark woman in a worn black wool dress answered the door and scrutinized us. Suzanne spoke to her—Madame Nair, of course, spoke not a single word of English. Then Suzanne and I were ushered into a large, musty room. In the room was a very old bed, a long table, a cupboard, an icebox, a cracked porcelain sink, and a small round table with several diminutive chairs around it.

Madame Nair gestured that we should sit down at the table. We did so and I placed the carrier gently on the floor between Suzanne and me, but I did not open it.

Madame Nair then brought us a plate on which were two apples and a knife. She left the plate on the table in front of us. I had no idea what I was supposed to do. Have breakfast? Or did they have some significance that was yet to be revealed to us?

Suzanne did nothing, so I did nothing.

Madame Nair then wanted to know what was the matter with the creature in the box.

I described to Suzanne what had happened, and she then translated it into French for the so-called gypsy woman. Who, as far as I was concerned, was about as much of a gypsy as I am a Rhine maiden.

Madame Nair listened and did not ask any further questions. She started to open the carrier. I leaned forward protectively but she signaled that I should sit back now and not interfere.

Our central casting "gypsy" woman plucked poor Bushy out of his carrier and held the large cat up as high as she could, handling his bulk as if he were no more than a wisp of a kitten. Bushy stopped wailing and looked down at Madame Nair in confusion and injured dignity. The Madame called out something to Suzanne in rapid-fire French.

"What? What did she say?"

"That your cat is a handsome specimen of the breed," Suzanne told me. "But he does not appear particularly intelligent."

I was furious. "Suzanne, you tell that woman that *all* Maine coons are intelligent—especially this one."

She merely patted me consolingly on the back.

Meanwhile, Madame Nair, still holding Bushy high above her head, walked slowly around the room studying him, turning her head, and then his, this way and that.

I decided I had made a dreadful mistake bringing my poor kitty to this lady. But Suzanne remained confident. I suddenly became aware that Suzanne was no longer standing by my side. I looked back at the table and saw her calmly peeling an apple. If I'd known a little more then about the French sense of humor, I might have guessed that Suzanne and the strange gypsy were playing some sort of practical joke on me.

For the first time since we'd entered the house, I got a good look at Madame Nair's face. She had a large birthmark on her face and neck. *Maybe,* I thought, *that is why they say she's a gypsy.* It was a red blemish that seemed to darken or fade in direct correlation with the strenuousness of her activity.

At that point, the old woman calmly walked over to the bed and placed Bushy on a pillow slip. She lifted him on it until he was at eye level. Then, using the pillowcase like a trampoline, she tossed him high in the air, where he flipped and clawed, and finally landed safely on all fours.

I let out a tremendous cry and yelled, "What are you doing?"

Paying no attention to me, she picked up the thoroughly disoriented Bushy and repeated the procedure.

"Stop that this instant! Stop it!"

She spoke to Suzanne, who purported to translate to me, but I don't believe I was being given a verbatim rendering.

"She says to calm yourself. It's important that she test the cat's balance if she is to make a complete diagnosis."

I sat down, miserable, helpless. Stranger in a strange land. I couldn't even look at the apple slice Suzanne was trying to press on me.

Madame Nair was finished with the trampoline test at last. She brought Bushy down to eye level again and launched a staring match with him. She poked and prodded him for a few minutes, and then at last placed him on the floor and walked over to where Suzanne and I sat.

Bushy seemed to be none the worse for wear. He just stood there gazing after the one who had turned him into a bouncing ball.

"There is nothing wrong with your cat, I think," she pronounced through the interpreter.

"Nothing wrong! But I told you—"

Madame Nair stilled me by placing her big bony hand close to my lips.

"Nothing wrong," she continued, "except a small upset of the digestive organs." She then actually waggled an accusatory finger at me and charged, through the interpreter, "You do not feed him correctly."

"Of course I do," I exploded again. "I spend good money on the best gourmet cat food in New York. It's what he's always eaten."

She smiled while Suzanne broadcast my defense in French. Madame Nair shook her head sadly as she listened. Then she replied, "In America, feed American food. In France, American food is no good. I will now end the disorder in your cat's stomach."

She placed a small dish on the table. She took two grisly, unboned, and unskinned sardines from her icebox and laid them carefully, almost reverently, on the plate.

"He won't eat it," I said. "I couldn't get him to eat anything at all this morning."

She ignored me completely and continued with her work—placing onto the sardines several drops of a clear liquid from a dusty, stoppered bottle.

She left her station once, to go back to the bed, where she lifted the mattress, extracted something, and then returned with a folded piece of newspaper. She unfolded the leaf of paper and dumped the contents onto the plate. "It is crushed Aleppo pine bark," she explained. Even when that was translated to me, I didn't know what it meant.

She set the plate down on the floor, halfway between us and Bushy. He walked boldly over to the dish, gave me one fleeting look, and then proceeded to eat as though I'd starved him for weeks. I'd never seen anything like it. He was finished with the sardines in seconds, pine bark and all, and was now frolicking on the bed, sniffing crazily at the pillow slip trampoline.

I thought the whole thing was utterly crazy,

but it was obvious I no longer had a sick cat on my hands.

I thanked Madame Nair profusely and inquired, through Suzanne of course, about her fee. After a prolonged conversation between those two, Suzanne turned to me and said, "She says there is no fee. However, she likes the scarf you are wearing . . . very, very much."

I happily handed it over.

It's funny. I know many people think that Provence is paradise. They work half their lives to buy a little house in a little town like Ste. Ruffin. It looked as if I *might* get to have one nice day here.

Crazy Madame Nair had cured Bushy and he was now safely back at the inn, rebonding with Pancho and telling him about the world outside the four walls of the cottage.

And Suzanne continued to be a wonderful friend to me. We shared a real blowout of a lunch at the town's ritziest restaurant. It was a meal I was happy to pay for out of my per diem. Then we went on a long walk during which she showed me the dunes and the salt bogs outside of the village, delivering, in her way, a proud lecture on the ecology of her adopted region of France. She even engaged in a little gossip about her neighbors, whom of course I did not know. But I thoroughly enjoyed it anyway. Mainly because it was so much easier to follow than the mile-a-minute show business tattle Mona Columbia had related to us.

So that one day was shaping up as a vacation from my vacation in hell. I went to my room to write a couple of cryptic postcards to friends in New York and get in a nap before dinner.

I dressed carefully that evening. I looked good when I joined the group in the dining room. I felt confident, pretty, perhaps even lucky—I had not utterly given up hope for the movie's prospects.

The first course was a delicious cream of asparagus soup.

We were seated unusually close to one another; for some reason the management had taken away several of the tables for that evening. The physical closeness gave the illusion of another kind of togetherness—almost like a family. Brian and Cilla were naturals for the parents, I suppose, even if in truth Cilla was considerably younger than I. Ray Allen and Claude and I were the adult children—some more adult than others, obviously. Sidney Rice was our great-uncle, who drank a little. And the grandchildren, or at least the younger kids, were Alison and Mona.

But the fissure in this family, the tensions, appeared very early in the meal, and it quickly became very ugly.

"This soup is kinda like the script," Ray Allen muttered and laughed bitterly to himself.

We'd all heard him, but no one responded.

"At least in LA they know what to do with a

goddamn asparagus . . . Why do they have to mash the hell out of everything in this dumb place?" His normally modulated voice had slipped into that all-purpose tough-guy register, loud and gruff. "Jeez . . . they can't stop screwing with things in this stupid country . . . like you couldn't stop screwing with the script."

Claude Braque quietly put down his spoon and addressed Ray Allen in an even tone: "What script do you mean, Monsieur Penze?"

"What script do you think I mean, asshole? The one you screwed up."

Why was Ray Allen talking about the script now? Had he heard the movie was being given a reprieve?

But his behavior suggested just the opposite. He was acting as if everything was definitely canceled. Besides—I thought the soup was anything but "screwed up." I thought it was wonderful.

"What do you object to in the script?" Braque went on, rational on the surface but obviously about to boil over.

"Aw, come on, man, cut the crap!" Ray Allen shouted. "What the hell is all that political garbage supposed to *mean*? My character just sits around spouting a lot of philosophy crap. He doesn't *do* anything anymore."

"The script was written in such a way—" Braque began.

"But *you* had to write it your way, didn't you? *You* had to keep putting in that phony intellectual stuff until nothing else was left.

You had to shape it around your own precious—French—*sensibilities*—and you know what I think of those."

"Perhaps you will have to tell me what you think of them, Ray Allen. I had not realized you knew what that word meant."

Penze first flung his soup bowl at Braque. Then he leapt over the table like a western movie villain and grabbed Claude around the throat. They rolled together onto the floor amid the screams of the onlookers—well, Mona was the only one literally screaming—and the shattering of glass and crockery.

Cilla Hood—"mom"—was the one who prevented them from seriously hurting each other. She grabbed the large paddle-shaped bread board from the table and managed to drive it between the bodies of the two grappling fools. Panting, they both looked up at her in astonishment as she stood wielding her insane weapon.

Braque and Ray Allen rolled clear of each other. Mona stood frozen in place. Brian had his head in his hands. Sidney Rice held a bemused little smile on his lips and both of the burgundies in his lap. I saw the proprietor dispersing the staff to begin the needed reparations. I had enough restaurant French to understand that he was ordering Josette, the little waitress, to bring out the rabbit pâté, our next course.

By the time we repaired to the lounge for after-dinner drinks, eight out of eight of us were stuffed and more than a little tight. After the blow-up, conversation was minimal; mostly we just kept eating and drinking as one course after another was placed in front of us.

All the goodwill and good hopes that had marked the day for me earlier were gone. I was once again in a most uncomfortable place—uncomfortable in every way—physically, geographically, emotionally, you label it. I wanted to lie down somewhere and kick my feet and scream like an enraged child. Mostly I just wanted to lie down. I had started to feel imprisoned in my clothing.

Mona Columbia's brightness was undimmed, though. Recovered from the dinner-table prize-fight, she seemed more vivacious than ever. She was living proof of the axiom that hyperintelligent women are attractive by any standard of measurement. The very air around her seemed to be crackling. Mona was wearing a short black leather dress that evening. It must have had a dozen zippered pockets. She reached into one of them and pulled out her notebook.

"Well, Alice," she said, "that was quite a little psychodrama, wasn't it? I bet you never dreamed you'd be doing a little bargain basement Pinter in the south of France. Though I suppose that's a bit of a redundancy, since any Pinter play is by definition cheap."

"A bad *imitation* of a Pinter play," I said, feeling guilty that I wasn't doing more to defend Pinter. I was allowing Mona Columbia's braininess to make a coward of me—I really hated that in myself. And she was taking notes now, which meant that something of what I'd say tonight was bound to wind up in some magazine. I felt the next thing to brain dead.

"I'm curious, Alice," she said. "Why does an actress like you do a movie like this one?"

"Money," I said.

"Yes, of course. Of course you're paid, but . . . someone like you . . . I just don't buy it."

"Buy it."

"Well, anyway, you know what Freud says about money . . . "

"Yes, I do. I also know what my grandmother said."

"What?"

"Money is a dairy cow by any other name."

"I don't think I get it."

"It's just a bit of farm girl humor, Mona."

She changed the subject without skipping a beat. "Did you know anybody on the project before you came over here?"

"No. I met them for the first time on the plane. Except for Brian. He—what?—recruited me in New York."

"I have the feeling, Alice, that in some strange way you're pretty objective about things. That's why I'd like you to answer this next question."

"Okay."

"Don't you think that in spite of their shortcomings, their excesses, their lack of insight, sometimes their lack of talent, film people—I

mean Hollywood people—are just more exciting to work with? Even *this* set of people?"

I laughed. "Is there something particularly
lacking in this set of people?"

"Yes, I suspect so. But that doesn't keep me
from finding them fascinating."

"You? I should think you'd be fairly blasé by
now . . . considering all the film people you've
been around."

"Not at all. They continue to amuse. Even
the dummies. Even the egomaniacs. Even the
hopelessly wiggy."

"Well, to be honest, I've been overawed by a
movie star or two in my lifetime," I admitted.
"Maybe in a way no New York actor could ever
overawe me."

"It's a little embarrassing, don't you think,
to be such a sucker for the mystique? I mean,
even someone as essentially vacuous as Cilla . . . " Mona nodded discreetly in Cilla's direction. "In her element she's probably dazzling. You see women like her hopping into
their BMWs on Rodeo and . . . oh, I don't
know . . . it's kind of ridiculous. But if Cilla
can make you feel like a hick, imagine what
it's like to talk to Myrna Loy, or Audrey Hep-
burn, or even Robert Redford."

"To give Cilla her due, she did manage to
break up that fight," I pointed out. "No one
else lifted a finger."

"Hmm. I suppose you have a point. Nobody
knows much about Cilla. For all we know, she
was a redneck lady wrestler or something before she hooked up with Brian." Mona stopped

talking just long enough to take a breath. "And you know who else is kind of interesting? That blond PA. Alison."

"What's so interesting about her?"

"She's just sort of spooky."

"Um hum."

"Though she is a tad self-conscious with it," Mona said, chuckling. "I mean, morning, noon and night with those shades of hers! And that far-off, homage-to-Dominique-Sanda gaze whenever she does take them off."

"It seems like a harmless affectation," I said, not knowing why I was sticking up for Alison Chevigny.

"She certainly seems to make *you* nervous, Alice."

"You noticed that, did you?"

"I watch people."

"For a film critic, you do quite a bit of psychological profiling, Mona."

"Yeah, well, it's part of the game. I'm part of the establishment media now. A kind of panderer, when you think about it. I can't just write about 'the work' anymore. I gotta give 'em the journalistic equivalent of tits and ass."

I enjoyed this woman tremendously.

"And don't you worry about a thing, Alice," she said confidingly. "I consider you a girlfriend now—not just a source for gossip or someone to bring down a peg. I don't have to mention you in my copy at all if you'd rather I didn't."

I appreciated Mona's confession of friendship, but didn't know whether I wanted to be

totally expunged from her coverage of the go-
ings-on.

Meanwhile, she had moved on to another
topic: Claude Braque.

"I can't make a convincing case that he's a
genius or anything," Mona said sheepishly.
"But one thing I can do with the power the establishment media gives me is throw a tiny bit
of credit to people like Claude for being good
at their craft. He knows as well as we do that
he isn't Godard. But I thought it would be nice
to make him the centerpiece of the story—for
once. As a wildly underappreciated actor,
Alice, you must know what I'm saying."

In my mind's eye I saw Mona's hand as it
brushed across Braque's neck. I said nothing.

Then she said, "Sooner or later, though, we
must get around to talking about Dorothy
Dodd, musn't we? I'd love to hear your take on
her."

My "take"? I didn't know how to take that
comment. "Well," I finally said, "she's dead."

"Yes. That seems to say it all, I suppose. The
lady is . . . dead." Mona set her glass down
then. And judging by the terrible weariness on
her face, all her energy was just suddenly
gone.

"So you met her on the plane, too?" Her
spirits seemed to pick up just a bit.

"That's right."

"Did you speak with her at all?"

"Sure."

"About what?"

"I don't know . . . the cats . . . the weather . . . she mentioned liking my dress."

"*Dorothy Dodd* admired your dress?"

"Yes, Mona. Or so she said."

Mona looked at me very severely then, almost as if accusing me of lying, as if it were impossible that Dorothy Dodd (who probably had owned more Armani suits than any other single living human being) might have paid me a compliment on my clothes. All I could do was smile innocently. But I was beginning to get the very uncomfortable feeling that this stranger from America via the French Riviera believed also that Dorothy Dodd had been murdered.

The trouble was, I also got the uncomfortable feeling that Mona believed *I* was the murderer. Maybe before this was all over, we'd have two lady investigators on the job.

"I think I'll go get myself a drink," I said in an apologetic voice, wanting to end this interview—or whatever it was.

In a moment of unexpected physical aggression, Mona blocked my way—just for a couple of seconds. Then she smiled self-deprecatingly, as if it had all been a joke . . . all some kind of interior drama that film critics are constantly enacting . . . a kind of wigginess, to use her word. I had no idea what it meant.

I didn't get a drink. I poured myself half a cup of black coffee and sipped it. But I didn't really desire that either. What I wanted was to just get out of there. So I abandoned the coffee and sauntered through the film people until I was safely outside.

I started walking purposefully toward my cottage.

"Alice!"

I turned toward the voice. It was Ray Allen Penze and he was calling to me from the steps of the inn. He came up very close to me. His two hands were spread wide in a gesture of abject apology.

He began his spiel with today's all-purpose word: "hey." It signaled apology, chastisement, tenderness, mere interjection, teasing, and ordinary greeting.

"Hey, Alice. I'm really sorry about what happened in there, man."

Why was he apologizing to me?

"That's all right," I said, and started to move away.

"No, I mean incredibly sorry. I mean, I . . . need a favor, Alice."

"What sort of favor?" I know my suspicions showed.

"You saw the way I acted in there. I'm going around the bend in this place."

Aren't we all? I thought.

"If I don't get a break soon I'm going to lose it completely," he continued. "There's a techie who's staying in one of the trailers. He's got a car he'll lend me. I just want to get away for a break."

"What does this have to do with me, Ray Allen?" I had become impatient with him and didn't much care whether I sounded unfriendly.

"I need somebody to take care of those cats

while I'm gone. Dot said you were dedicated to cats."

You need somebody to take care of those cats even when you're here, I wanted to say.

"There's plenty of food and stuff in the place. Enough for an army of cats."

"How long will you be away?"

"I don't know—a couple of days."

"And when did you want to leave?"

"Now. Yesterday. I want out of here bad. I've just got to get away from these people for a while."

I wondered which people he meant. Just Claude? What about Sidney Rice? Was Penze one of those Brit haters Sidney had talked about? For all I knew, Ray Allen wanted to get away from stuffy, sober, stagy, judgmental old me.

"Will you watch them for me?" he asked insistently.

"Yes, of course."

"Great! Hey . . . thanks . . . really. I appreciate it."

I didn't reply.

"You know, I'm not exactly the badass people say I am."

"That's nice to hear."

He started back toward the inn.

"Just a second, Ray Allen." I knew what I wanted to ask him. I wanted to say, "You idiot, don't you know that one of Dorothy's cats is America's feline sweetheart? Don't you know that Maud is worth millions in residuals?" But all I said was, "Any special instructions?"

He looked perplexed. "What do you mean?"

"You've got three cats in the cottage. Is anybody on a special diet or anything?"

"They eat what you put down."

"What about medicines?"

"They're all healthier than I am."

"Is there *anything* I should know about them?"

He seemed to be digesting my words carefully. Then he said, "Once in a while, two of them get into a fight."

"Which ones?"

"How should I know? They all look alike. Dot didn't even give 'em names. She said all cat names are human names, and that cats give themselves their own names, but it takes many years to find them out . . . or something like that."

I soon stopped trying to decipher what he had been trying to say. The important thing was, he genuinely did not seem to know about Maud.

"I never saw you perform in New York," he said, switching gears. "But I heard you're something special. I was looking forward to working with you."

"I don't think it will come to pass."

"Hey, we're not dead yet. And even if it doesn't happen this time . . . You know, I just feel it. We could be dynamite together. Especially the love scenes."

Hmm. Once a gigolo, always a gigolo.

"Actually, if you wanna know something,"

he admitted, "I thought the script for *Emptying* wasn't half bad. Did you like it?"

"It had its moments."

"Great part for you."

"You think so?"

"Yeah. A mature role."

I grinned. But he couldn't see the grin. It had grown too dark out. And for some reason the floodlights on the inn's beams had not yet been switched on.

"Thanks again, Alice. Gotta go," he said, flying off.

I went toward Maud's cottage. Why not start my cat-sitting assignment immediately?

The three Abyssinians were waiting to be fed. I hated to admit it, but Ray Allen was sort of right—I was unable to tell which one was Maud until I pulled all their legs to see which one yawned. Then, when I had rediscovered her, and when all three had eaten, I sat on the bed and played with her, letting her yawn and roll over to her heart's content.

The other two cats, when Maud was frolicking or rehearsing, seemed to look on with a bemused contempt, like workers whose boss was a benign idiot. When she wearied of her games, Maud just lay next to me, staring up at me as if I had some important information to dispense.

"Dorothy's not coming, guys," I said slowly. "Best to hear it now and get it over with."

At the sound of Dorothy's name, the other Abbys leapt softly onto the bed. After a few minutes tickling and belly scratching, they seemed to have enough attention. I got up to leave.

But for some reason I just couldn't walk out. I felt their eyes on my back. And when I turned they really were staring at me—all three of them. With the kind of anticipation that cats always exhibit, the kind that used to drive me crazy because I didn't know what they were anticipating, what they wanted, what they needed.

"What is it, beauties?" I asked them.

They remained as they had been, but their eyes had turned hard. They were glaring at me now. Unforgiving. Because in not finding out who murdered Dorothy, I had thrown in my lot with the murderers.

The darkness outside . . . the dim cottage light . . . the six eyes boring into me. For a minute I thought I had crossed over into that land where humans and cats talk freely to one another and the humans truly believe the others understand. I had a quick, awful vision of myself as an eighty-year-old woman wearing fingerless gloves, smelling bad, and floating through the alleys with my shopping cart full of cats.

I had to get out of there.

"You guys wouldn't dare treat Madame Nair this way," I said to the kitties. "'Cause she'd take you and throw you six feet in the air and then drop you—boom!—on that terrible old bed of hers."

I laughed at the memory of Bushy's startled expression under Madame Nair's ministrations. I was sure she would love to get her hands on these three.

Why, she'd grab a little Aleppo bark and mix it with a little pickle relish and . . . and . . .

I stopped that silly line of thought, and silently apologized to Madame Nair.

What a fool I'd been not to see it before this minute.

Whoever murdered Dorothy Dodd to get their hands on Maud would be very unhappy indeed to learn that an ailing Maud had been turned over to some dotty gypsy herbalist.

Wow, was this going to be simple. *And* elegant. It was going to be the easiest, quickest, most direct trap I'd ever sprung.

6

I did not leave my cottage for breakfast that next morning until way past eight because I had to be sure that they were all in the inn. I had to make my announcement in front of as many as possible.

When I did start walking toward the main house I noticed that Mona Columbia's distinctive red sports car was not in the lot.

Where had she gone? Had she left during the night? Odd. Penze had left last night, too. Was there something between them? I grimaced. I'd already speculated about affairs between Mona and every male on the premises. It was getting stupid. But I just couldn't keep up with or even understand the nuanced moves of that young lady.

A moment before I entered the breakfast room I put on my mask of grief. It was a mood I could always handle. It was a role I loved to play.

The juice had barely been served to me when Brian Watts asked, "Is anything the matter, Alice? You don't look so good. I mean, you look . . . worried."

"It's the cats."

"Your cats are sick?" Cilla asked.

"No. Dorothy's Abyssinians. Ray Allen asked me last night to take care of them while he was away."

"What's the matter with them?" Alison Chevigny asked, blowing delicately across the surface of her coffee.

"They're vomiting something awful. Temperatures seem up. And a lot of trembling in the limbs. Two out of the three of them, anyway."

"It sounds like the DT's," Sidney Rice said.

"More like an allergy," said Claude Braque. "Maybe it's the feathers they use in the beds. I heard that some people are allergic to goose down. I've never met an American who wasn't allergic to something."

"These aren't people, they're cats," said Brian.

"What are you going to do?" Cilla asked.

Brian answered for me. "Don't be stupid, Cilla. What do you do when you have a sick cat? Take it to vet, of course."

"Well," I said, "it's not that simple. There are no vets around. And the cats are too sick to be moved now. I thought I'd wait another twenty-four hours. If they don't get better, I'm going to ask Madame Nair to come over. I don't want to. But I guess I'll have to."

I was met with an assortment of blank stares.

"Who the hell is Madame Nair?" Brian asked.

I laid it on very thick. "Well, she's sort of this gypsy animal doctor. She uses all kinds of bark and roots and who knows what else. I heard that people in the village trust her . . . but of course, what choice do they have? Personally, I think she sounds more than a little touched."

Alison spoke up. "What do you mean by 'touched'?"

"You know, a bit mad. But I understand she cures more often than she kills. Isn't it crazy?"

"Must be a stitch," Sidney muttered. "Especially for the animals. Poor sons of bitches."

"Maybe you ought to wait until Ray Allen gets back before you do anything like that," Brian suggested. "They were Dot's little beasts. I guess he should decide."

I shrugged. "I will wait, as I said. For twenty-four hours. If he's back, fine. If not, fine. I'll call in the voodoo vet. I don't see what choice I have."

"Anyone seen Mona?" Cilla asked, as if it were important that the film critic witness these unfolding events. Perhaps Cilla thought the controversy over the sick cats would make good copy for Mona's article.

But no one seemed to know where Mona Columbia was. We returned to our breakfasts. I surveyed my audience surreptitiously. I thought I had played the role pretty nicely.

One of the people at the breakfast table probably had murdered Dorothy Dodd because of her millionaire cat. And that person was not going to stand for the idea of my taking two of the look-alike Abyssinians—one of whom might very well be Maud—to a gypsy for some bizarre treatment. He or she would not chance it, considering what was at stake. Some time this evening, I knew, he or she would take Maud out of that cottage, out of the incompetent cat-sitter's grasp, and out of the reach of the infamous Madame Nair.

I spent the morning watching Suzanne Aubert paint. Then I went back to my room and kibitzed with Bushy and Pancho. During the afternoon I made several visits to the three Abbys and read my Michelin guide to the region. I even practiced some French conversation, trying it out on Bushy, who was fluent in nineteen languages, including ancient Ugaritic.

As dinnertime approached, I readied myself for Act II of the one-woman play I was putting on. I wanted to fine-tune the trap.

"You're looking better this evening," Brian commented as I sat down for my soup—a luscious seafood bisque.

"How are your cats? Any better?" Claude Braque asked.

"Not hers," Cilla corrected him. "Dorothy's. Yes, how are the little things?"

I hesitated before answering, gauging the level of audience interest. "Not that much better. They've stopped vomiting, but they still seem feverish. And the trembling hasn't gone away. I don't want to take the chance. I'll get the gypsy first thing in the morning."

For a moment, the room was silent save for the clinking of spoons against soup bowls. Well, the trap was fully baited now. It would be sprung tonight.

At the now-traditional after-dinner coffee and brandy hour, I tried to be upbeat, to circulate among the folks. And incidentally to look for any signs that any one person seemed particularly nervous.

Perhaps because Ray Allen was absent, as well as Mona, there was none of the usual bustle, not to mention the almost combative tension. All present seemed calm. But maybe that was just because they were all despairing of Brian Watts's ever raising the money for the movie. Maybe they were all just exhausted and wondering what they should do next.

Anyway, about nine-thirty I wandered out and headed for Maud's cottage. The Abbys had already been fed and they seemed quite happy to see me.

"Tonight's the night, Maud," I said to the star as we went through her dramatic exercises of yawning and rolling.

For some reason, the other two cats seemed impatient with the proceedings. One even swiped at my leg-pulling hand. I blew on her little ear and she ran off in a huff.

"It may get a little hairy, Maud," I told her and took her into my lap, "because, let's face it, some bad person is going to try to kidnap you tonight. But stay calm. Remain calm at all times, okay? Don't resist. Remember, I'll be watching, and I'll make sure you're safe. Understand?"

They all seemed to understand. That, or they didn't give a damn. Maybe after being cooped up in that cottage for so long they were longing to be absconded with. Even by a murderer.

I went back to my room. Bushy was fast asleep on the bed. I thought I heard Pancho in one of the closets. I pulled the rocking chair over to the window, placed my travel alarm clock on the window ledge, and set it for a little past midnight, just in case I dozed off. Then the alarm would wake me, I would set it for two hours hence, and thus I had a fairly good plan to remain at least intermittently awake and watchful.

It would be better if I could read during the vigil, I realized, but then the criminal would see the light in the cottage. So I began my watch, seated in the rocker, my eyes on Maud's place, bundled in sweaters. The wind outside was beginning to pick up and it whistled around the corners of the buildings like mad motorists.

It didn't seem that I was in France. It didn't seem that I was waiting for a murder suspect. But that was to be expected. After all, I was probably the only one other than the killer who knew the accident that had taken Dorothy's life was no accident at all. And I didn't really *know* that. In all the cases in all

the histories of criminal investigation, I might
have been sitting on the most circumstantial.
But that had never stopped me before. Besides, when all was said and done, a multimillion-dollar kitty was residing incognito in a
nearby room. Just waiting to be plucked.

The time went by quickly. I was having no
problem staying awake. That is, until my
clock read eleven-thirty. Then I promptly fell
asleep and was awakened by the alarm
around midnight. I reset it for two A.M and resolved to keep my eyes open. Why had I gone
to all that trouble, all that acting, all that trap
baiting, if I couldn't even do the minimum
work to spring it.

The wind had died down. Once in a while I
heard wings whooshing by. They might have
been bats or owls. I was tempted to rouse the
cats, who would have been most interested in
the avian life going on outside. But I didn't
wake them. Bushy slept on, occasionally making a little peeping noise in his sleep. Pancho
was snoring in one of the open suitcases.

I gradually increased the intensity of my
rocking, and soon I had drifted off into a
rather lovely state of limbo, neither asleep nor
awake, where each movement of the chair
seemed to bring back good memories that
washed over me, memories of cats and things.

It was one fifty-five when I saw that sliver of
movement. Mind you, that was all it was—a
sliver—and for the first time since this whole
mess began, I found fear. It was sudden and
paralyzing.

Why? I didn't know. I didn't even know if the sliver of movement was significant.

I got out of the chair and pressed my face against the glass. My entire body was trembling. Yes, someone was there. Someone was around and about Maud's cottage. But the moon had vanished and all I could make out were changes in the darkness.

I waited awhile. Then I saw another quick movement. This time the door to the cottage was opening. Then, just as quickly, it was shut again.

My God, this was it! I could hardly breathe.

I started out of my room, but stopped abruptly. A weapon. I needed a weapon, protection. I was very likely about to confront a murderer—a thief at the very least. I should have some sort of weapon. Another instance of my not thinking far enough ahead. Damn it!

I looked around the room wildly. What could I use? What? I surely had no gun, no club, no knife—there wasn't even a poker in the old fireplace. I could find nothing. And time was fleeting. I rushed over to the writing desk. Yes. The inn had provided a souvenir letter opener embossed with a drawing of the church in the square. It was not made of steel. But it was sharp to the touch. It would have to do.

I held it prominently in my hand and opened the door. I slinked across the grounds until I reached Maud's cottage. I pressed myself against the outside wall, like they do in all the commando movies. I listened. Yes. There was no doubt of it. Someone was inside.

I walked silently, slowly, to the cottage door. The letter opener weighed so little. I had the desire to prick my palm with it, just to test it again.

The doorknob was ice-cold. I was sweating and freezing at the same time. So this was the fabled south of France. I might as well have been in Albany.

I took a deep breath, as if I were about to recite the opening poem at the inauguration of the president, turned the knob, and stepped inside.

I flicked on the light switch and thrust my weapon straight out in front of me.

Standing by the bed, looking at me stonily, was Alison Chevigny.

One of the velvet-lined cat carriers sat on the bed, its top flipped open. Inside it was Maud. She didn't seem the least bit distressed.

The thief was glaring at me angrily, almost self-righteously, as if I were exhibiting the worst kind of manners in interrupting her.

"What are you doing here, Alison?" I put as much authority into my voice as I could muster.

"What does it look like? I'm taking the cat out of here."

"And why should this cat concern you?"

"You look here, I'm not going to allow you to take her to some ridiculous quack vet. Besides, there's absolutely nothing wrong with any of these animals."

"I asked why you think the cat concerns you, Alison."

"All right, *Miss* Nestleton. If you must know what I'm doing here, I'll tell you."

Her voice had taken on a hard American edge.

I waited. But her bravado seemed to suddenly disintegrate. She sat down on the bed next to the carrier. She reached inside it then and stroked the great lady's ears.

"I am here," she said quietly, "to take back what belongs to me."

"What is it that belongs to you?"

"Piaf."

"Piaf? What is that? You mean Edith Piaf? I believe she is long dead, Alison."

"This cat. This cat is Piaf."

"And she's yours?"

"Yes."

"Are you sure of that? Are you sure that's your cat? What about the other two Abyssinians? Why not one of them? Why must it be this one—Maud?"

"I know very well which she is. This is Piaf. And she belongs to me. To me and my husband."

She looked completely forlorn sitting there, and not very much like a murderer, I had to admit. Still I felt there was some aura of menace about her. I did not relinquish my grip on the weapon.

"If this cat is yours, how did she come into Dorothy Dodd's possession?"

"We sold her to Dorothy two years ago. My husband and I lived in a village near here. Dorothy was vacationing there. She had traveled all around Provence. Hugh, my husband, wanted to work in films. That's all he lived for . . . fantasies about writing and directing movies. But nothing ever happened for him. Hugh was raised by circus performers and had worked with big cats—lions and tigers. He had developed this gift for training house cats. And he taught our Abyssinian kitten how to yawn and roll over and jump through hoops—many things. It was a way to keep himself busy when he wasn't fantasizing. Teaching Piaf. He found it amusing."

She brought both hands to her face suddenly and with great passion, as if some memory was just too much for her. Then she pulled her hands away and continued.

"Dorothy was entranced by our kitten. She said she had two kittens of her own in the States. And she wanted Piaf. She told Hugh that she thought there might be money to be made with a charming cat who knew so many tricks. She said that if anything ever came of it, we'd get half the profits. Hugh had been out of work for months. We didn't have a dime. We sold Piaf for two hundred dollars. And we never heard another word from Dorothy again. We never received anything from Piaf's career as Maud."

I heard a sound outside the cottage and immediately tensed into a defensive posture. It might have been her husband, her accomplice, outside. What if he came in? I doubted a letter opener would cut much ice with a lion tamer.

"Where is Hugh?" I demanded.

"Dead. He committed suicide last year. He hung himself."

"It was revenge then," I said.

"What revenge? What are you talking about?"

"You killed Dorothy because she, in a sense, killed your husband. Isn't that why?"

"I did *not* kill Dorothy. She was killed in the van. Are you crazy?"

"Don't count on it. You and I both know that wasn't an accident."

"I don't know any such thing. But I do know that I didn't come here to murder her. I read that an American film company would be coming to Ste. Ruffin to make a movie and that the executive producer was Dorothy Dodd, who was traveling with the company. I disguised my looks a little so that she would not recognize me. I got the job as production assistant. My idea was to steal Piaf back. But I lost my nerve. And Piaf seemed so happy."

I didn't believe her story and told her so. "It's too perfect," I said.

"What is?"

"Your sad tale. It has all the elements. A husband tragically dead. A little kitten whisked away by a nasty witch. A promise not honored. Everything but the hounds nipping at your rear end, to quote another cynic. Do you really expect me to buy all that?"

"I don't care what you buy. Believe it or don't believe it. Call the police if you like. Do what you will."

"But I don't know how you did it. You were driving the van I was in. You had no contact with Dorothy from the moment we left the airport."

She did not reply.

"Of course, you were probably working with someone riding in her van. Was it Ray Allen? Braque? Did you promise them a cut of Maud's earnings? But you must have known that once you stole Maud she would no longer be a gold mine. You could never hope to deal with the sponsors yourself, because they'd know you'd taken her. No, it must have been just your hatred for Dorothy. You hated her because of your husband's suicide. And you wanted her dead."

"That's ridiculous. Dorothy did a terrible thing to us, but no one can say that was the only reason for Hugh's suicide. And anyway . . . oh, why don't you put that stupid knife away!"

"It's not a knife. And I'm not going to put it away because I think you're dangerous, young lady. I think you're a murderer."

"I am not."

"So you say."

Alison sighed. She closed her eyes and kept them that way for a moment. "Look," she finally said, sounding tired, "I didn't do it. But even if I had, I don't think you'd turn me over to the police."

"Oh, really? Why is that?"

She stood up slowly. I kept the opener

pointed in her direction, but she shrugged it off as if I were holding a toy.

Then she did a very bizarre thing. She pulled off her hair clips and let her astonishing golden hair tumble down.

This was the second time I had seen her hair loose, and I was even more disturbed by it this time. And again, I didn't know why it was so upsetting.

"Go on," she said. "Look at my hair. Look at it very carefully. And then take a good look at me."

"I know what you look like, Alison."

"No. You don't. You really don't. Because if you knew what I looked like, you'd know who I am."

I said nothing. What was there for me to say?

She sat down again, her hands moving through her hair.

"You must know . . . who . . . I am."

"You're not making any sense, Alison."

"I am your sister's child."

I laughed at her. "What an idiotic thing to say. I don't have a sister."

"But you *did* have one, once."

My laughter stopped. All at once I was lightheaded. The dizziness just swarmed into my head and then cleared out again.

"You listen to me," I said weakly. "I have no sister."

"Her name was Gem."

I dropped the letter opener and felt feebly for

the edge of the bureau. I needed something to hold on to.

"I am Gem's daughter," Alison said deliberately, loudly. "I am your niece, Alice Nestleton."

How long had it been since I'd heard that name? Gem. At least thirty years, perhaps more.

"I am Gem's daughter," she repeated, over and over.

"Stop it! Stop it!" I screamed. And then the room was dark and twisting and it was as if I were down, down in a bottomless Minnesota well.

When I opened my eyes I was staring at the three Abyssinians on the bed beside me.

"Are you all right?" Alison said.

Her hair was pulled back now. She held a glass filled with water gently to my lips and helped me to drink from it.

"Well," I murmured, "this is all a bit—"

"Yes, it must be."

"You see, if you are who you say you are, my grandmother had sort of banned the very mention of your mother's name."

"I *am*. Believe me. My mother's name was Gem Nestleton. She was raised on a Minnesota dairy farm by her grandmother. She had a younger sister named Alice. They both had long golden hair. My mother died a few years ago in a hospital in California." She looked at me intently and added, "But I don't know why my mother's name was banned. I never knew what happened between her and Gram."

"Oh, dear. You dear girl." I pulled her to me and held her close then, and we both began to cry. The cats came closer and pushed their curious little faces up to ours.

Then I held her away from me and looked searchingly into her eyes. Could this all be true? Was she really my sister's child? It was such an astonishing turn of events. All the villages in all the seacoast towns . . . and she had to show up in this one.

"Please," Alison said, "tell me what happened to my mother. What happened on that farm when she was young?"

"I don't know much."

"But you know why Gram did not speak her name."

"Yes. I know. It's something I haven't thought about for a long time. But I remember."

She waited patiently for me to go on. Piaf had draped herself across Alison's knees. The other Abbys hopped off the bed and went their separate ways. Across the room the letter opener lay on the floorboards, where I had dropped it.

It wasn't easy to bring those memories back, but the lovely face of my niece seemed to demand it . . . and I fought hard to summon them up.

"I was six years old when Mom and Dad died. Your mother was fourteen. We went to live with Gram. She had a beautiful old farm in dairy country.

"It was hard at first for us. We loved Gram and she loved and cared for us. But your mother—Gem—never recovered from her grief, I think. From what had happened to our parents."

The memories were coming back in waves now; hideous memories, sights, sounds. Panicked, bleating animals, burning animal flesh, the charred remains of a farmhand. All terrifying.

But what I said to my niece was, "Your mother set fire to the barn. Many of the animals died. And a man was killed—burned to death. Your mother was sent away from us. And Gram refused to even mention her name again. Ever." I squeezed Alison's hand tightly.

She smiled sadly. "My mother never told me about any of that. She always spoke of the farm with affection. But she never said why she left. I am not surprised at what happened. She was in and out of mental institutions for as long as I can remember. And we were always moving. I don't remember my father very well at all. He left us. When I finished school I had to get away from my mother. I loved her, but I knew she would swallow me up someday—destroy me. I went to Paris to study, at film school. And that's where I met Hugh. He wasn't a student. He lived in the same rooming house."

"What was your father's name?" I asked.

She didn't answer. She stared past me. I realized that there really had been no father in the familial sense . . . that she was just parroting a tale about the father who deserted them. Maybe Gem hadn't even known who the father of her child was.

"Why did you wait so long to tell me who you were?"

"At first, I just couldn't believe it. It was too strange that you would be here. That you would actually be here making a movie. And my mind was on poor Piaf . . . getting her back. Then, once I accepted that it was you, I kept trying to talk to you . . . and you kept avoiding me. As if you were frightened of me. I thought you hated me."

"I'm so sorry, dear. It's just—well, perhaps it was some buried memory of Gem . . . of her hair. I don't know."

"You seemed to recoil from me."

"Yes. I'm not denying it. From that moment I saw you here with your hair down, I knew something was happening. But I couldn't come to grips with it."

Alison lifted Maud, who was really Piaf, and shook her playfully, making her wave her little paw. "This is my aunt Alice, Piaf. Say hello!"

But Piaf said nothing. Maybe she needed to be given one of those esoteric signals before she would say hello.

"You know, our little Piaf has another talent. Hugh taught her how to sing. Isn't that right, Piaf? Her big number is 'Je Ne Regrette Rien.' But only when she feels like it."

I noticed that every time she spoke the

name Hugh there was a great deal of love and grief adhering to the word. I wanted very much to hear more about him, about their love and their life together. But I knew she would tell me only when she was ready . . . when she truly felt at ease with me. I kept silent.

We tickled and teased the delightful cat for a few minutes more. Then a sudden cloud came over Alison's face. "You won't bring in that dreadful woman from the village, will you? I don't want her to even touch Piaf."

"The wicked witch of the Camargue, you mean? The one who destroys kitties and pups with a single wave of her herbal wand." I was joshing my poor niece, but she didn't seem to get it.

"No, seriously," I explained, "first of all, there was never anything the matter with any of the cats. It was just a story I made up. And second, that woman in the village, Madame Nair, is no charlatan. She knows her stuff."

"You mean you said that to trap someone?"

"Yes."

"And look at who you caught. Me."

"Look, indeed."

"I swear to you, I had nothing to do with Dorothy's accident—or murder—or whatever it was."

"No. I know you didn't, sweetie. Don't worry."

Maud had the most commodious cottage on the premises. We all stayed there that night:

Alison and me, Piaf and her two stepsisters, and the dim, sad spirit of my sister Gem.

The morning dawned brilliant, the sun like a chisel scraping the night away.

Alison and I left the cottage and walked hand in hand down into the village, through the deserted streets, and onto the wharf.

A single fishing trawler was visible on the water, its nets still hung on the mast, like aquatic spiders.

"I've made a friend in the village. Her name is Suzanne. She paints here every day and sometimes we go to the café together. I know you'll like her."

"I'd love to meet her."

I found myself staring at Alison from time to time, when I was sure she wouldn't notice. It was an impolite thing to do, but I had the belief that each time I looked at my niece I would come closer to reconstructing Gem's face. I could only recall the separate elements of it— the high forehead, the beautifully formed mouth—and, oh, what lovely hands she had. My older sister. I had adored her.

"Look! Look up there!" Alison called.

Three gulls were circling together in a kind of dance, riding up on the wind currents and then falling, soundless, never touching but always close, almost breathtakingly close.

We walked along the shore, toward the great dunes, buttoning up against the rising wind. The shore birds in all their variety dipped and strutted and ran before the incoming tide. Alison bent occasionally to pick up a blue stone or an ivory shell.

"Isn't it beautiful here, Aunt Alice? Do you see why Hugh and I loved this area?"

I did. I had never felt so calm or happy. One minute I had no family, and the next minute I did. There was no longer that sense of being a stranger in a strange land. I was at home.

"That looks like a good one," Alison said, pointing to a monster stone at the waterline. I waited while she collected it, and looked back casually toward the wharf.

I could see a woman standing alone there. She had what might have been an easel under one arm. I guessed that she was contemplating where to set up.

"Let's go back, Alison," I shouted. "I think I see Suzanne."

We hiked back to the wharf. It *was* my friend standing there. But she seemed not at all interested in us. She wouldn't even acknowledge our presence, even though I'd started calling her name when we were fifty yards away.

When we got closer, I understood. North of the wharf was a knot of people on the beach. They had surrounded an object washed up on the shore.

"It's probably a pilot whale," I told Alison. "They often, for some mysterious reason, make suicidal rushes onto the beach and die there. No one can explain it."

Suzanne raised her hand to silence me. I was profoundly insulted.

Then she walked off toward the chattering group of people. She motioned that we should follow. She left her easel and paint box there on the wharf. Just let them drop.

Suzanne was walking very quickly. It was not easy to keep up. A steady knocking sound was reverberating in my ears, louder than the crashing waves: my heart.

We stopped about ten feet from the crowd.

"Not a whale," Suzanne said coldly.

No.

Mona Columbia lay naked on the beach, bloated, blue. Her head had been crushed. It was horrible.

7

We sat dumbly in the café. The place was not yet open officially, but the proprietors had kindly made it available to the police who had come down from Arles and to all those who had seen the body and needed solace.

I was so dazed by what I had seen that I proceeded to act as if I had seen nothing. I introduced Alison to Suzanne Aubert as my niece and then went into a long story about how we had discovered each other . . . how wonderful it was . . . how, against all odds, we both had a family again.

Obviously, both Suzanne and Alison knew I was in a kind of shock; they just allowed me to babble on. I was soon exhausted, though, and sat silently in my chair thinking of that beautiful and incredibly vibrant and smart young woman lying dead.

Then a handsome older gentleman sat down at our table and lit a cigarette.

"I am Inspector Lucas, from the prefect at Arles," he said.

As I turned to face him, I could also see that my coworkers and the staff from the inn were arriving. Everyone looked washed out and scared. Sidney and Ray Allen and Brian and Braque—with Cilla Hood sadly bringing up the rear. She was carrying, of all things, a thermos. I guessed that it did not contain coffee. My coworkers did not sit down. They gathered and then dispersed at the front of the café, sometimes darting out to stare at the ambulance that held the corpse of Mona Columbia.

Sidney nodded in my direction. There was great kindness in his eyes along with his fear. I tried to return the greeting, but couldn't be sure my head was working.

The inspector finished his cigarette before speaking again.

"I have had a few words with your colleagues," he said. He had a very thick accent and spoke impeccable diplomatic corps English.

"They have been unable to tell me where Miss Columbia had been the past day."

"I cannot tell you either," I said, my throat constricted. "I last saw her thirty-six hours ago. At the bar in the inn. When I woke yesterday morning, her car was gone."

"Yes," he said. "The car has not been located as yet."

Two of his assistants came over, younger men dressed in wool-lined jackets. They appeared to be reporting their own findings to him. I didn't know. While the inspector listened, the proprietor brought over an espresso and set it down in front of him. Lucas smiled his thanks. He drank the coffee in a single gulp and his eyes seemed to brighten. The two young men left.

The inspector gave us the abbreviated version of what he'd just been told. "Someone in the village, a fisherman, saw the red car at one of the technician's trailers. At least he thinks it was the car. He is quite old."

Then the proprietor, as if understanding that we too needed a boost of some sort, brought three more coffees to the table—one for Suzanne, one for me, and one for my niece. It was still amazing to think of Alison Chevigny as that . . . my niece.

Another policeman approached Inspector Lucas and leaned down near his ear to say something. When Lucas left the table for a few moments, Suzanne told me that she'd heard part of the report: they were still looking for the car, but Mona had mentioned to someone that she'd rented it in Marseilles. They were checking on it.

Several men entered the café then. I recognized one or two or them, and then realized they were the technicians who remained in the trailers after Brian Watts's first cut. They were supposed to clear out shortly.

The men were ushered to a rear table, where they sat, visibly uncomfortable, defensive. A young policeman called one of the technicians out and led him into the kitchen.

The interrogations, I presumed, were about to begin.

There was a hubbub in the room, a constant, excited chatter. In addition to the police and the technicians and my film company colleagues, there were village residents wandering in, alarmed and demanding information. Others stopped to stare in through the windows.

Inspector Lucas rejoined us. "As one might imagine, they are not used to murder here in the village," he commented. "It has been many years since one occurred. I think in 1971. A German tourist."

"No, not true," I corrected him.

He was understandably surprised, but allowed me to go on.

"There was a murder much more recently than that. Only a few days ago."

"Do you mean here, madame—in Ste. Ruffin?"

"Yes, I do. Near the church outside of the village."

"Do you speak of Madame Dodd?"

"That's right."

"But Madame Dodd was killed in an automobile accident. It may have been a preventable one. But nonetheless an accident."

"No," I insisted. "Murder."

Lucas regarded me for another moment, then turned to Suzanne and said something that I naturally did not understand. I knew he was asking my friend if I was rational. Suzanne herself looked at me with a question-

ing glance, as if she too had her doubts, but
then, if I was reading things correctly, she ag-
gressively assured the inspector that I was indeed a woman to be listened to.

Lucas asked me in a matter-of-fact tone,
"You have just seen the body of the young
American, have you not?"

"Yes, I saw . . . Mona."

He nodded sadly, thinking, I'm sure, that
my horror and shock at the sight of Mona's
corpse explained the kind of statements I was
making. A minute later he excused himself politely and left the table.

Both women turned excitedly to me when he
was gone.

"You did not tell me that Dorothy Dodd was
murdered!" Suzanne said urgently.

"No. I didn't tell you," I said. "And I didn't
tell you that she was murdered because of a
cat."

Then I backtracked. "At least I *thought* she
was murdered because of a cat. Now I
think . . . well, now I don't know what to
think. Except that Dorothy and Mona—in a
sense—inhabit the same grave."

Dinner, that night at the inn, fell apart very
quickly—and all of us with it. We had survived
Dorothy's murder and the withdrawal of the
production funds, but we could not, as a
group, survive the battered, naked corpse of
Mona Columbia.

Brian Watts had obviously come unraveled.
He refused to sit down for dinner. Instead he

prowled the dining room making obnoxious comments about the woodwork and the tatty curtains and the service at the inn. Cilla, usually able to help him out of any situation, just stared bleakly after him, occasionally righting some object he had tipped over in making a point.

Sidney was staggering drunk. He kept clutching at the waitresses, begging them in schoolboy French to lend him a car so that he could get out of this insane asylum.

Our director, Claude Braque, had gone totally silent. He had retreated so far into himself I didn't know whether he'd ever come back. Halfway through the meal he got up and wandered like a ghost back to his quarters, never saying a word to anyone.

As for Ray Allen Penze, he seemed calm enough, but he had reverted to an even more childish posture than usual. He sat making paper airplanes with the pages from an address book. I don't think he realized how obvious it was that he had been crying all evening.

Feeling we were the only sane people in the room, Alison and I left the table as soon as we'd eaten. The cold evening air was preferable to all that unhappiness in the main house, no matter how inviting the fire in the hearth.

I walked over to the wrecked van and began to circle it, becoming more and more agitated.

"Aunt Alice, please calm down!" Alison finally took hold of my arm and pleaded.

I laughed uncomfortably. I knew time was running out for all of us, for all my theories.

"You see," I told her, "I am sure that Dorothy was murdered. But I don't know how. All I know is that she went into a van, refused to put her seat belt on or adjust the rearview mirror, and then did and said some strange things once the drive began. Like saying that it had rained . . . washing the windshield." I stopped my narrative at that point and stared at my newfound niece. "Do you really want to hear the ravings of your crazy aunt?"

"Yes, I'm interested."

"All right. If she was murdered, I thought, then it must be because of the cat your late husband trained. The cat the world called Maud, whom I discovered quite by chance. That was why I set the trap. Happily, I ended up trapping you. We ended up finding each other. But it meant that Maud was not the rationale for the murder. No murderer showed up."

I paused and stared at the shattered windshield. "So perhaps Dorothy was not murdered. Oh, there was that possibility. And I probably would have accepted it. But then comes the murder of Mona Columbia. And you must realize how mysterious it all is getting. She claims to be writing a piece on Brian Watts. But the moment she gets here I begin to notice all kinds of hidden alliances and affections. Something else is going on with the young woman. A lot more is going on than just writing an article."

"Then you think there was a connection between the two murders—if Dorothy was murdered."

"There *is* a connection. There has to be. The mistake I made was thinking that Maud was at the center of everything. She never was. And so I am left in a very bad position."

"How so?"

"We're never going to make this film, Alison. The company is dissolving quickly. We'll be scattered all over the world in a couple of days. There's no time for an investigation. And Inspector Lucas won't conduct one because he doesn't believe that Dorothy was murdered."

"You sound as if you've dealt with this kind of thing—with murder—before, Aunt Alice."

"I have. If not always successfully."

"I thought you were an actress."

"I am, I suppose. To the extent you can be an actress when you have nothing to act in. I mean, yes, of course I'm an actress. But I also take care of people's cats. And once in a while, when something comes up, I'm paid to investigate. . . . " I didn't complete the sentence because someone banged noisily out of the dining room at that moment.

It was only Sidney. He stumbled past us on the way to his cottage.

"Do you think he's going to be all right?" Alison asked, watching him as he disappeared into the darkness.

"I'm sure he'll manage."

"Go on, Aunt Alice. About the murder. Don't you agree with the police that one of the technicians might have killed Mona? After all, she was apparently in one of the trailers. Her car was seen there."

I corrected her gently but firmly. "No one saw Mona there. An old man saw a red car that might have been hers. It doesn't mean anything. But to answer your question: no, I don't agree with the police. I believe someone involved with the film is the murderer."

"So what will you do?"

"I've got to find a link between Dorothy Dodd and Mona Columbia. Any kind of link."

"How? Where will you look?"

"That's a good question."

I felt the fever growing. Yes, I was down, but not out. I was late, but the door was still open a crack. Maybe there was enough space for the truth to slip in.

"Tell me, Alison, there must be a major library in Marseilles, correct? Someplace a person could conduct a bit of scholarly research? It would have to have English as well as French language sources."

"Yes, a very good one."

"Then you're going to Marseilles."

"What for?"

"To be my scholar. To be my legs. I want you to compile a bibliography of Mona's writings. You could do that, couldn't you?"

"Of course. But you said there was little time. If I have to take the train . . . "

"You'll be in Suzanne's car, I hope. And so will she. She worked for an international bank with a branch in Marseilles. She can get me a business profile of the great entrepreneur Dorothy Dodd."

"Are you sure she won't mind?"

"I've had the most incredible luck with finding friends on this incredible trip. You and Suzanne. She's played the role of fairy godmother very well up till now," I said. "Let's ask her if she's willing to continue."

We walked quickly toward the village.

8

Suzanne and Alison left early the next morning. Suzanne's car, an old Citroen, was long past its prime and far past the ministrations of even the most talented mechanic. But it still chugged along and, she assured me, could maintain respectable speeds when flogged.

Ray Allen Penze had become a very scarce commodity. I didn't know where he was spending most of his time or what was taking up all his attention. I just knew it wasn't the cats. The poor things were being shamefully neglected, I felt. So, without being asked, I took it upon myself to act as their guardian. I spent my day shuttling between my cottage and Ray Allen's, tending the two sets of cats.

I avoided the main house all that day. I didn't even go in for morning coffee. At mealtimes I walked into town to the café, which was still abuzz with the slaying, even though the police investigators from Arles were no longer so visible.

I spent much of the day in my room, reading or just sitting in the rocking chair. I felt like the town busybody, watching the comings and goings of the others. The depression and bewilderment were apparent on their faces as they went in and out for meals or to make phone calls or fetch drinks, as they left the grounds and returned. Everyone was making his own arrangements for getting out, going home. They all seemed to be sleepwalking—especially Claude Braque, on the one or two occasions he showed his face.

As I'd told Alison, I didn't have long. I had to make a move soon, or the suspects would all disappear.

And still the crushed van hulked there, malevolent as ever. Like a memorial to the doing of evil and the cheating of justice.

Never had I felt the passage of time so acutely. As each rock of my chair ticked away the seconds, I felt that all chances to solve the murders were dribbling away. I had nothing. I had no single connection between them. The removal of Maud from the center of the storm had sucked out all reason. I had no motive from which to work. So I waited, rocking. I hoped that Alison and Suzanne were driving carefully. But I also wanted them to hurry.

What was I reading? A very strange little book that my friend Tony Basillio had insisted I bring along. It was Brecht's *Manual of Piety*, a collection of poems translated by an American. Basillio was a severe Brecht "freak." Of course, it was Tony's stage sets for some of Brecht's plays that had garnered him his highest professional acclaim. So perhaps his Brechtomania was self-serving. I had always loved Brecht's plays as well—had a part once in a production of *Jungle of Cities*—but I had never read his poetry qua poetry.

There I sat in my rocking chair in the murderous Camargue, reading a bilingual edition of Bertolt Brecht. That struck me suddenly as funny and crazy *and* pretentious *and* sweet, all at the same time. Oh, well. If I'd ever found myself in weirder circumstances, I didn't recall them.

One poem fascinated me immediately. It is called "Early Morning Speech to a Tree Called Green." And it is simply about a man who watched a tree sway in the wind at night, thought it reminded him of a drunken monkey, then in the morning apologized to the tree for such a thought. The man goes on to tell the tree that he understands that it, like he, is in mortal struggle all its life against alien forces, and also like him is alone in a mass civilization neither of them can deal with.

At least that's what the poem seems to be about. It is written in some of Brecht's loveliest yet most bitter language.

Not only did I find the poem oddly mesmerizing, but I began to read the original German on the facing page. It came rather easily to me. And then I remembered that I had taken German in high school. Yes, I had. And the pronunciation came back. And the grammar. Soon I was reading it almost effortlessly, proud of myself, happy, and I wondered how many other things about high school I had forgotten.

All I could recall of the school was that it was a small dismal block building sticking out yellowish from the flat Minnesota farmland. And then I saw a few faces in my head—classmates.

Then, suddenly, I saw another face—that of my sister. So clear and real and stark that I cried out and leapt from the rocker to begin walking back and forth, pacing, my arms folded and my eyes closed.

It was her lovely face *that* night . . . that terrible night. I could see my grandmother, too, confronting my sister. Gram was enraged. Screaming. Terrifying. She was pointing toward the charred shell of the barn . . . and the corpses inside it.

And my sister Gem, her face calm, innocent, had the slightest hint of a smile on her mouth. She must have been mad . . . completely psychotic. She had probably been that way always except for brief interludes. And now she was dead. And because of an old woman's horror and hurt I had just shut my sister out of my mind and my life. She was like a book I'd finished and didn't want around anymore . . . or a dress now out of fashion. I had completely forgotten about her.

The pain cut so deep that I flung myself onto the bed and pressed my face into the blankets. Oh, yes, paradise in Provence. The days in that lovely French cottage had truly become hell. I fell into a black sleep.

It was Bushy who woke me, after the sun had gone down, with his strutting and fretting. He wanted attention, stroking, and food. I gave him all three; Pancho as well, as much as he would stand still for. Then I went to take care of Dorothy's little ones.

They were being perfectly feline: happy enough to see me but certainly not effusive. Like many beautiful creatures—actors included—they had an air of absolute entitlement . . . to love, to affection, to admiration and indulgence. There *are* worse ways to go through life.

The great Maud did not solicit any yawning or rolling over. She rubbed up against me prettily in thanks for a good meal, but she seemed always to be looking past me . . . waiting for someone else to arrive. Not Ray Allen Penze. Who was nowhere to be seen.

I detoured onto the parking lot as I made my way back to the cottage. It was cold and damp. The night wind was like a musical line, rising and falling and always increasing in speed. My hair, which I had not tied up, was blowing in the wind.

What an ugly, obsessive object that van had become for me. I knew it was the key to Dorothy Dodd's murder. Yet I had nothing even approaching a coherent explanation for its role in the killing. Let alone the role it had played in crushing the life out of the singular and beautiful Mona Columbia.

I had only the little pieces having to do with the van—the rearview mirror, the seat belt, the windshield wipers, all of Dorothy's strange behavior. But all those little pieces were worthless without an understanding of the big picture, as the film people liked to say. And the big picture in this case—the hook, the high concept—was that one of the passengers had managed to kill Dorothy without the others' noticing. I knew how impossible that sounded. Perhaps there *was* no coherent explanation.

In my room, I drew the cats to me and we waited together for Alison and Suzanne—my operatives, so to speak—to return from the big city.

It was not until ten-thirty in the evening that I heard the moans of the ancient Citroen outside the cottage. I ran to the window. The car lights were out so as not to cause undue distress.

The moment they entered the room I knew they'd found something. My words to them had been: "There is little time and probably a lot of material. What I'm looking for is the event that stands out, that makes you question, that opens up a connection or the possibility of one."

I knew they had understood when they left and I knew they had succeeded when they returned.

I had an orange for each of them and we all sat on the bed as they peeled the fruit. When she had finished hers, Suzanne rose and stretched. Then she handed me a folder.

"They were very cooperative, very kind to me. Here is a photocopy of everything they had in the research department. There were many articles about Dorothy Dodd in different papers and magazines from all over the world. And some information I probably should not have."

I opened the flap of the file folder. As I flipped through it my heart sank. I had not expected merely a news clipping service to be the prime mode of research for an international bank. After all, many of these articles were probably planted by Dorothy's own PR firm. I knew that the egos of entrepreneurs were matched only by the egos of rock stars.

Suzanne saw my disappointment and vigorously waved it away. She leaned over and leafed quickly through the pages in the folder until she came to two sheets of paper fastened with a clip. She pulled these out of the file, took the folder away from me as if it were no longer of any importance, and then gave me the two sheets.

I studied the first page carefully. It was a chronology of Dorothy's business activities that had appeared in a Canadian newsweekly in 1990. Most of the stuff was pedestrian—firms she had started up, firms she had taken over, lectures she had given at Harvard Business School, and so on.

But the entry for 1984 was quite interesting and a bit different from the others.

It showed the bandit side of Dorothy Dodd.

In 1984, Dorothy, it seemed, had been involved in a nasty business venture in Canada involving the publication of a magazine. It was one of those magazines that purported to identify all the coming trends in fashion, theater, food, etc. It had the best writers, it paid big salaries, it featured beautifully done graphics, and had extremely high production values.

And it soon folded.

The "autopsy" on the magazine found that the books had been cooked, fraudulent stock had been issued, and circulation figures consistently faked. Dorothy had narrowly escaped criminal prosecution.

But two of her associates were sent to prison.

It was a stunning revelation. Dorothy as aggressive—yes, that was obvious. As careerist? Yes, that was obvious, too. As ruthless. I could buy that as well. But a criminal? That was something else again.

The other item Suzanne had selected for me was also something new, and much more intriguing.

It was a piece about the growth of hypochondriacal symptoms among the general populace because of so much medical and drug advertising making people aware of the existence of symptoms and diseases they had never heard of previously.

The article went on to talk about "famous hypochondriacs," mentioning an assortment of athletes, politicians, movie stars, and business tycoons—including one Dorothy Dodd. It went on to say that she was notorious for checking herself into the hospital at the slightest hint of illness. Her staff, the article said, had had to learn to live with this peccadillo.

I looked over at Suzanne. She was beaming. Yes, she should be proud of her research prowess. She had totally changed my conception of Dorothy . . . from woman of the year to neurotic hustler. It was a startling change in so short a time. But it only confirmed with greater accent that she had been murdered.

Then it was my niece's turn to show off. She triumphantly pulled out of her canvas bag a rumpled computer printout. Alison carefully unrolled all three feet of its length.

"Mona was certainly a writer," she said admiringly.

She held up one end of the stack of paper and I picked up the other. I began to read the bibliographical listing for Mona Columbia.

Most of the work consisted of articles using the kind of neo-modern critical babble in the titles that I am sure only other very hip critics understand. The pieces had been published in forums such as *Cineaste* and *Partisan Review* and *Cahiers du Cinema*. Several articles of a more popular nature were published in *Playboy* and *Premiere* and *Rolling Stone*. They must have been written when Mona needed to finance a trip, I surmised. There were dozens of individual film reviews for a host of newspapers and magazines on both sides of the Atlantic.

So many listings. So many. My vision began to blur.

"Take a long look at *this* one," Alison said, guiding my finger to a single entry. I blinked away the blurriness and focused.

My finger had come to rest on the listing for an article published in *Interview*. A long interview—appropriately—entitled "Wild Life/Wild Talent: A Conversation with Ray Allen Penze." The date was April 1990.

One of those funny chills went through me. I could tell that Mona had erotic fish to fry in Ste. Ruffin. The first night here she seemed to exhibit that; to display all kinds of mysterious attachments beyond her stated literary one with Brian Watts. But I really thought it was Braque she was after. Even though it was obvious that Mona had left the inn the same night Penze had. Even then I didn't really put two and two together.

I looked proudly, gratefully, at my two assistants. I gathered Sir Bushy to me and hugged him fiercely. For a moment there I was very happy. What a great job the two of them had done—and on such short notice—two women who probably had never in their lives even contemplated tracking down a murderer. They had honed in on what I needed to crack the case. They had done their job with dispatch and imagination.

It was Pancho who managed to puncture my

feeling of triumph. He had interrupted his running hither and thither just long enough to stare at the group of us in the middle of our papers and orange rinds. He had that typical alley cat cynicism on his battered face. He actually seemed to be laughing at us. Then he ran off again.

Pancho was right: so what if Dorothy had been eccentric and ruthless? And so what if Mona and Ray Allen had been lovers, possibly since 1990?

If the two of them had killed Dorothy, how had they done it? And who had killed Mona? Ray Allen? Why? Why would he get rid of Dorothy in order to be with Mona, then turn around and get rid of her?

There was a set of sobering facts, memories, that still had to be reckoned with.

I remembered that immediately after Dorothy's death Ray Allen Penze had taken part in a drunken soccer game.

After the terrible discovery of Mona's body the very same Ray Allen Penze was making paper airplanes like a bumbling idiot.

Was he a cold-blooded killer? Was he on drugs? Did violent death mean nothing to the man? Or was he that cliché—an actor whose ridiculous roles had overwhelmed him—like Ronald Colman in *A Double Life?*

I had to admit that it was just as possible that Mona's interview with Ray Allen was simply that, an assignment. Perhaps she had not given a thought to him in the three years since. Her winding up in Ste. Ruffin at the same time he was here might have been utter coincidence.

Damn it! There were too many lines of inquiry and too little validation. I saw Alison refolding the printout. And too little time!

I looked squarely at my pretty young niece.

"Alison, did you sleep with Ray Allen Penze?"

Everyone was embarrassed by my outburst—everyone, including me. I hadn't known I was going to ask such a rude question . . . but I had no wish to take it back.

Alison flashed a hurt look my way, a little anger in it, too. I knew what she was thinking: that I was accusing her of a liaison with Penze, perhaps saying that she knew something about the murders and his part in them, maybe even saying she'd had something to do with the killings.

I had to admit, those things had flashed into my mind. Maybe I was afraid that the same kind of madness that flowed through my sister also flowed through her daughter. Blood to blood, as they say.

But then again, the same insanity could have me in its grip.

Our eyes locked. I repeated my question.

"Why are you asking me this?" she said defiantly.

"Because I . . . because you should tell me if you did. You must."

"I'm an adult, Aunt Alice. By rights, I should not answer you. But I will. The answer is no."

"But he wanted you to, didn't he?" I persisted.

"Yes. But what of it? I'm a grown-up. I don't fall prey to every man who's attracted to me. Ray Allen probably tries to sleep with most women he meets."

Somehow I couldn't leave it at that. I pressed one final time: "So are you saying you don't find him the least bit attractive?"

"Oh, for heaven's sake," she said, laughing. "Yes, I suppose he's attractive. But the only man here I was at all interested in was Sidney Rice. He, however, behaves as if I don't exist— or as if I'm a mere babe in the woods."

I wondered then what her husband Hugh had looked like. Alison had not shown me a photo of him or talked about his physical appearance. Perhaps he'd been some sort of father figure to her, as well as a husband. Lord knows that wasn't unusual for young women with troubled pasts.

"Of course, I suppose Mr. Rice would only be interested in someone older than I," she said resignedly, and seeming very much like a mere babe.

"Not necessarily, dear. Just ten years older and aged in an oak barrel."

By her giggle, I judged that she had forgiven me.

I had bought a nice bottle of wine in town and I asked Suzanne to open it. While she was pouring drinks for us, I went over to the window and stared out at the dark night. My sudden suspicions about Alison had been just a tangent. No, all the threads were still tied to that van and what transpired in it on that particular day.

Weren't they? There were now so many possible combinations, so many possible scenarios. I had a trio now . . . a triad: Dorothy, Mona, and Ray Allen. Two out of three were dead. Nonetheless, they were connected. Somehow connected. Somehow hooked into Dorothy's past. Perhaps to her Canadian misadventure? Perhaps to her neurotic hypochondria?

Another chill went through me as I stood peering out into the night, unable to make out the wrecked van. I reached for the brocaded throw on the back of the rocker.

Suddenly I recalled something Inspector Lucas had said. Not his exact words, just an impression of them. He'd said them in reference to Mona's sporty red car. He'd said that she'd told someone the car had been rented in Marseilles.

That hadn't registered at the time—right after the shock of seeing her body. But now it seemed quite strange and pregnant with all kinds of possibilities.

Because, first of all, I found it peculiar that nowhere in Mona's entertaining tale of her recent travels did she even mention Marseilles.

And second, there was the car itself. Mona's car was a vintage model Triumph. Probably something a wealthy collector would love to own. Why would an ordinary rental car outfit handle a vehicle like that? The problems with such a car would surely be legion—far too much trouble.

Did those things have any meaning? Were they just silly contradictions?

But if the death of Dorothy Dodd was all wrapped up in that hulk out there—as I was sure it was—then why shouldn't Mona's fate also be tied up with her vehicle?

"Suzanne, do you think your car is up to a trip to Arles in the morning?"

There was a twinkle in her eyes. "*Mais bien sûr*, Alice. It is immortal."

"It had better be, because Citroen is no longer in business."

"Why do you want to go to Arles?" asked Alison.

"To speak with the inspector."

"I thought you might say that," Suzanne said, helping herself to more wine.

I could not seem to shake the chill. I pulled the woolen throw tighter across my shoulders.

"Aunt Alice!" Alison called in an alarmed voice. "You have the strangest look. What's wrong?"

"Two out of three," I said.

"What does that mean?" asked Suzanne.

"It means," I said, running to the door of the cottage, "I'm worried about Ray Allen Penzel!"

It was one of those sudden inspirations—a burst. What that final chill in my room signified was the realization that if Ray Allen was the third party in that deadly triangle that included Mona and Dorothy, then his life was also in danger.

The reason we hadn't seen him lately was that he'd already been killed.

I signaled that Alison and Suzanne should stay put and I went to find the corpse.

Wrong.

Penze was alone in the lounge, vodka in hand. He was in a foul mood, surly, pacing. Before I could get out a word, he warned me that if I was there to make a call, I'd better "forget it." I couldn't use the phone, he said, because he was waiting for a call from his agent in LA.

I asked after the three Abyssinians—had he found them well when he returned? He looked through me as if I were one of the holes in his carefully pre-ripped T-shirt. He did not say good night when I left, and I didn't bother to speak to him again.

So much for my burst of investigative inspiration.

In my room again, I kissed Alison and Suzanne good night and turned in, not expecting it to be a good night at all. But there was the promise of Arles.

9

Arles, a city of some 60,000 souls, had been one of the jewels of the Roman Empire, Suzanne told me as she wheeled the Citroen expertly through the old city. That was not so hard to imagine. I rubbernecked constantly as we tooled past the Amphitheater and the great cathedral of St. Trophime and the medieval ramparts. That much heralded Van Gogh light sparked off the gray stones.

It was as though Suzanne were reading my mind. "It's a shame," she said, "that your time here is taken up with such terrible things. You should be enjoying this wonderful part of the country. Come back in the summer, Alice, and I will show it to you properly."

How I wanted to do just that. I wanted to stand on the Pont du Gard. I wanted to see the Palace of the Popes in Avignon, the cathedral at Nimes, to walk the tree-lined boulevard in Aix-en-Provence . . .

But of course there was no time that day for a tour of any kind. We had to focus on the business at hand.

The three of us walked boldly into the *hôtel de ville*, which housed the prefecture. I tried to imagine a police precinct in New York being located in a château. It had the makings of a one-act absurdist play.

Inspector Lucas appeared not at all surprised to see us—a function, no doubt, of his invariable good manners. In fact, he behaved as if it were perfectly normal for the three of us to be sitting in his office, pressing him for more information on the murder of a woman we barely knew. After we assured him that we were all perfectly comfortable on our chairs and wished no coffee or tea, he lit a cigarette and, without further ado, began his summation in a matter-of-fact voice.

"Miss Columbia was killed with a blow to the head. A single blow from a very heavy object unquestionably made of metal. It was not a hammer but more likely something like a tire iron.

"She had not been *violé*—raped, that is— though her clothing was removed. Most probably in an attempt on the murderer's part to make it appear that the assault was of a sexual nature.

"She was dead at the time she was placed in the water, somewhere north and west of Ste. Ruffin. The murder took place approximately twenty-four hours before her body was discovered."

That meant that Mona died not long after she vanished from the inn.

"Tell me, Inspector," I said, "have you found her red car?"

"We have not, madame."

"Are you trying to?" The moment I uttered those words I was sorry. I realized immediately how accusatory they sounded.

Lucas, however, kept his even, polite posture. "Oh, yes, madame. We are trying to find it."

"Because," I added placatingly, "it is critically important that you do find it."

"Ah. How perceptive you are, madame. Yes, we agree it is important that we find the automobile. Please accept my assurances that we are making every effort."

"If I might take just a few more minutes of your time, Inspector . . . "

"But of course, madame."

"I have been bothered by something you said the last time we met. I wonder if there could have been some mistake."

"My wife often says the same thing. What is it that troubles you?"

"You said you had learned that Mona rented her car from one of the agencies in Marseilles."

"*Oui.* That is correct."

"Inspector Lucas, I encountered Mona when she first arrived in the village of Ste. Ruffin. She drove up to the café in a wonderful-looking red sportscar—a Triumph T4 that had to be more than twenty years old."

He nodded. "Very observant of you, madame. And . . . ?"

"Well, rental car agencies deal in inexpensive new cars, do they not? It seems very unlikely they would rent a car that is almost an antique."

The inspector smiled and said something to Suzanne in French. He spoke too quickly for me to get even the gist of his comment. He paused, obviously waiting for her to translate for me, but Suzanne seemed reluctant to do so. She looked downright embarrassed.

It was Alison who ended Suzanne's discomfort, making the translation herself. "Monsieur Lucas said he realizes that Americans might find it strange that a company would deal in things that are not new. But some things that are old have their own special value."

I nodded my understanding to the inspector and refrained from any backtalk.

"The company is helping us in the search," he said, switching back to English. "Naturally, they want the car returned. Indeed, the manager is quite upset. He has told one of my men that he will continue to charge the daily rate until the auto is returned, whether Miss Columbia is living or dead. Of course, it is only his anger speaking. I've told him that Miss Columbia's estate would be responsible for six days and six days only—no more."

I leaned forward a little then. "Six days?"

"Why, yes. The total number of days the car was in her possession."

"Are you sure about that?"

"It is not a matter of my being sure, madame. The rental agency's records show it. They checked her passport and airline ticket before assigning the car."

"Airline . . . did you say airline ticket?"

"Yes, madame."

"Inspector, are you by any chance saying that Mona Columbia was newly off the plane from New York when she rented that car?"

"Absolutely, madame." He lit another cigarette then and reclined somewhat in his chair. "You know, madame, we have not been successful in discovering the whereabouts of the car, but our department has always had a fine reputation for the small details of police work. I have confirmation from the airline's passenger list right here in my desk."

Lucas's statement had shocked me so much that his refined sarcasm rolled right off my back.

So Mona's "on the road" travelogue had been a fabrication. She had arrived in France only the day before the film company landed.

What had been the point of all those lies? And what else had she lied about?

My mind was racing. I was dimly aware of Alison speaking to Lucas. When I could focus enough to listen to what they were saying, they switched back to English.

"Does that mean the technician has been exonerated?" she was asking.

"Yes. Luckily for him. Unhappily for us. We have shifted our suspicions onto . . . other parties," Lucas answered craftily, hinting that someone else might soon be arrested.

Suzanne and Alison waited in silence for me to ask further questions of the inspector. But I had no more at the moment. This new revelation about Mona had shown me what kind of swampy ground I was operating on. What I thought was rock-solid truth could be sheared away at any time.

We didn't talk much on the drive back. We arrived in the village in time for a late lunch at the café. Not that the awkward two P.M. hour would have presented that much of a problem in terms of eating. If one is resourceful enough, one can find *something* to eat in France no matter what the time.

I ordered a small endive salad and a chicken sandwich.

"I don't think they will ever find that red car," Alison said, digging into her croque madame. Having eaten in any number of up-scale Manhattan coffee shops, I was familiar with the croque monsieur; but I'd never heard of a croque madame. It turned out to be a French dip topped with a fried egg. I figured Basillio would appreciate it.

"Oh, I think they will discover that car," Suzanne said confidently, cutting into her little eggplant pizza. "That Inspector Lucas is a smart one."

My lunch was delicious, but I wasn't paying very much attention to it. There was a dressing on the salad I could not quite identify.

While Suzanne and Alison continued to talk about Lucas, I went on thinking about what we'd just learned.

Why *had* Mona constructed that bogus story about her travels? I didn't like any of the possible answers to that question, as they all pointed to her involvement in Dorothy Dodd's murder. Had she killed Dorothy in league with Ray Allen . . . because of him . . . in spite of him? But she had been nowhere in sight at the time of the crash.

" . . . he reminds me a little bit of Robert." Suzanne laughed self-deprecatingly.

"Who is Robert?" I asked.

"My husband."

Suzanne's eyes were suddenly glistening with tears.

Alison began the instinctual gesture of reaching over to clasp her hand, but then she stopped herself. I could see that she, too, was crying. Certainly about Hugh.

I had an odd, almost ridiculous reaction to the sight of the two of them weeping over their dead husbands. I was jealous. I wanted to have a dead husband for whom I could weep.

I overcame that, however, and placed a comforting hand over each of theirs. "For some reason I think of Hugh as being very thin. Was he?" I asked, trying to lighten the mood.

"Imagine a paper clip. Now unfold it. That was my skinny Hugh. But he had an enormous appetite."

"I have never liked skinny men," said Suzanne, drying her eyes.

"Oh, but you would have liked him," Alison replied. "Hugh was the most wonderful person I've ever known. He was kind, he was intelligent, he was . . . a bit crazy, too. More than a bit. But the best person in the world." Her face turned bitter suddenly. "Just the kind who wind up killing themselves, aren't they? The world is no place for them."

"Had he really worked in the circus?" I asked.

"Yes. His family had been in the circus for generations. His father and grandfather both trained big cats. Lions mostly. Hugh said they don't have many tigers in French circuses. He never knew why."

I fiddled around with my salad. The fact was, I didn't feel very well. My head and stomach were churning. And of course Mona was still on my mind. Murder was on my mind.

Still, I felt I needed to play the kind auntie. "Well, dear," I said to Alison, "Hugh was obviously a genius with house cats as well. Look at the wonderful job he did of training Maud."

"He was good with all animals. He loved them all. But cats especially. He used to say that you can't really train a cat. They are smart enough, but not really interested in pleasing you. That is their genius, he said. They are our equals."

"But he did train them," Suzanne noted.

Alison chuckled, sadly. "Not really. Well, only in a way. It was very strange to watch. He waited until they had, naturally, done what he wanted them to do. And then he talked to them. He implored them. He gave them goodies. It was a kind of romantic operant conditioning—very strange. But believe me, it worked. And then he would transfer the act to some kind of signal. Like pulling a paw. Oh, he was so gentle and so persistent and . . . unrushed. It took a long time. It was fascinating."

"And you say he taught Maud to sing?" I asked, not genuinely interested.

"Not Maud. Piaf."

"Yes. I meant Piaf."

Suzanne laughed derisively at the thought of a singing cat.

"No, it's true," Alison told her, laughing also. "I wonder if she still remembers her song."

"What song is that?" Suzanne asked, playing along.

"What do you imagine the song would be with a name like Piaf? It was 'Je Ne Regrette Rien,' of course."

Suzanne sent peals of laughter through the café. And then, in a full, dusky voice, sang the opening bars of the famous song, à la Edith Piaf. It was not a bad imitation.

But I was only half listening to their merriment. I knew I was down for the count on this case. This was one murder—make that two— that would not be included in *Nestleton's Greatest Cases*, a figment of Tony Basillio's imagination.

I hadn't acted wisely or quickly enough. I'd squandered the time and resources of Alison and Suzanne as well. Why, for instance, had I asked for a ride to Arles? Couldn't I have phoned Inspector Lucas instead? Of course I could have. Had I expected Mona's red Triumph to be sitting in front of police headquarters, just waiting there to give up its secrets to me?

"And what did it sound like?" Suzanne was asking Alison.

"To be honest, Piaf the cat did not sound like Piaf the Sparrow."

"I am shattered," Suzanne said, laughing heartily.

"It was really a series of squeaks and meows. And Hugh would first put on the record and then start singing himself—he was no singer, either. Finally, Piaf would join in with him and the real Piaf. It was quite a racket. But soon Hugh didn't need the record to get the cat started. He and Piaf would just sing duets."

Through her laughter, Alison started to cry again, and she stuck her knuckles into her eyes the way a very little girl might. She choked back the tears and threw her head back defiantly. "I would give anything to hear that racket again."

"Did your little Piaf learn any other songs?" Suzanne asked in a kindly voice.

Alison shook her head. "No. Time ran out on Hugh. And a very bad lady destroyed, in a sense, his hope. Hugh lived on hope."

We ordered coffee and sat silently drinking it. The afternoon sun had vanished, leaving faint shadows to crisscross the table and floor.

Alison broke the silence. "That Abyssinian loved Hugh so much. When Hugh would work late into the night . . . I'm sorry, Aunt Alice. You, too, Suzanne. I'm talking too much, aren't I?"

"Not at all, Alison," Suzanne assured her. "Go on."

I was still thinking, blaming myself, feeling foolish. But I resolved to try to pay closer attention to my two tablemates.

"Well, Hugh wrote these crazy screenplays, you see. That were going to make him a cinematic lightning rod . . . take the art of film one step further. And little Piaf used to sit so calmly on the table where he was writing. She was so intense. As though she were urging him on. She stayed with him for hours."

Alison's audience of two gave appreciative smiles.

"Once in a while, she would even give him a little kiss."

"A kiss?" Suzanne said. "Do you mean the cat?"

"Yes. Well, we called it a kiss anyway. I couldn't really be sure. But it was adorable to watch. Hugh would be writing and Piaf would be watching, as usual. Then, on the spur of the moment, she would get up, stretch her beautiful body, walk close to him, and press her nose against his forehead. Then she would take her seat again."

"How charming! She kissed the way the Eskimos do," Suzanne noted happily.

"No," I put in, "Eskimos kiss nose to nose."

"I never believed that," Alison said. "Anyway, I know it was a kiss. I'm sure of it."

"And what would Hugh do?" asked Suzanne.

"Nothing really. He went on writing. When he was concentrating on something there could have been a nuclear attack and he would not notice."

"You mean he didn't return little Piaf's kiss?"

"No."

"Ah ha," Suzanne teased. "Like the real Piaf—always giving more than she received. Piaf the kissing, singing cat has had quite a full life, hasn't she?"

"It was her yawning on cue and rolling over that made Dorothy Dodd millions," I said.

"Yes. But it was the kiss that really told you who our cat was," Alison said testily.

I looked at my niece, a bit startled by her sudden display of anger, as if she thought Suzanne and I were making fun of her memories.

Then, right then, I remembered something. A kiss. A different kiss. And the memory so riveted me that I pressed my hands together and must have uttered some kind of sound . . . as though I were in pain. I had to react quickly to avoid knocking my sandwich to the floor.

Suzanne and Alison looked at me with worry on their faces.

"I'm fine, I'm fine," I told them. "It's just that I remembered something about that day . . .

that day we landed in Marseilles. When we stepped off the plane."

I remembered a kiss. I could see it unfolding again.

Ray Allen Penze and Dorothy Dodd kissing passionately at the airport. They had embraced suddenly and wildly, like the impetuous, innocent young lovers they decidedly were not.

That was a kiss full of heat and abandon. Unashamed. It might even have embarrassed the onlookers a little. It was not at all like little Piaf kissing Hugh. No, not at all.

And how out of keeping that kiss had been with Dorothy's cool, composed, woman-of-the-world exterior.

It was a kiss that had to have been initiated by Ray Allen.

"A kiss of death!" I hadn't even known I'd said it out loud until Alison asked, "What did you say, Aunt Alice?"

"I need a little air," I said, already on my feet. "I'll be back shortly."

I walked quickly down to the wharf and stared out at the water. That kiss. That killer's kiss. Kiss of death. For the first time I had an inkling of method. I felt that I knew what had happened.

The gulls were swooping and soaring. Swooping and soaring.

Yes, Mona and Ray Allen were lovers.

There was an older woman, who could buy anything.

Yes, I had the motive.

I had a scenario for murder.

One rebel gull went honking just over my head.

But how could I be sure? How could I break this thing open? And how could I know that Penze and Mona were the only ones involved?

The cold air was oddly bracing. It made me feel strong and smart.

There was a way to nail this case. But it was dangerous. And illegal. I was in a foreign country. I would be dealing with Inspector Lucas, ultimately, and I didn't know the limits of his indulgence.

I turned away from the water and started walking quickly through the village like a monk saying his prayers, arms folded, head in chest, mind focused. Was it another false burst that I'd just experienced? A fantasy?

I knew I was making a big leap in fixing on a theory of the murder based on so little hard evidence. But what else could I do—time was so short. I had to go forward with the kiss of death idea or forget the whole thing.

Suzanne and Alison were just as I had left them.

"Feeling better?" Suzanne asked.

"Much better. And I must ask yet another favor of you, Suzanne. After everything you've already done."

"Of course. What do you need?"

"It's a little more complicated than a car ride, I'm afraid."

"All right."

"First I want to say, Suzanne, that the only

reason I ask this favor is that I think I know how and maybe even why Dorothy Dodd was killed."

She waited, not saying anything. Alison began to breathe faster.

"But a great deal of the puzzle is still missing," I continued. "The corner pieces, however, can be put into place by us. And once we find those pieces, we can also know who murdered Mona, and why."

"I believe you," Suzanne said simply.

"Good. Is there a pay phone in the café?"

"Yes. Near the kitchen."

"Very good. What I need you to do is place four telephone calls."

"That is the favor?"

"Yes, that is the favor."

"To whom do I make the calls?"

"Ray Allen Penze, Claude Braque, Sidney Rice, Brian Watts."

"Your coworkers on the film, you mean . . . at the inn."

"Precisely. I want you to call them one by one from the phone here in the café. Around the time we're having dinner at the inn tonight."

"And what shall I say to them?"

"That you are calling from the American Consulate in Marseilles. Identify yourself as Simone—Simone something—make up a last name."

Alison and Suzanne exchanged confused looks and then looked back at me.

"Tell each of them," I said, "that you are the

assistant to the vice consul and you're calling at his request."

"Alice, I . . . I cannot," she said quietly. "It is dishonest."

"I know. I'm sorry."

"It is also probably illegal," Alison added.

"Yes. That it definitely is," I confirmed.

"But why do you ask me to do this?"

"Suzanne, please, just first listen to what I want you to tell them. The message will be the same for each man. Three simple points—"

One of the aged proprietors of the café stopped at the table, checking whether we wanted anything else. We all smiled and declined. I waited until she was out of earshot.

"Three points. *Number One:* the cremation of Ms. Dodd's body has been postponed. *Number Two:* Ms. Dodd's family will have their own physician with them and they are demanding that the French authorities permit a private autopsy upon their arrival. *Number Three:* tell each man that his presence is required at the consulate within seventy-two hours to supplement the police report on the accident."

Suzanne drew a deep breath, about to speak, but then she fell silent, obviously giving grave consideration to what I'd asked her to do. There was tremendous distress on her face.

Alison seemed equally uncomfortable, fidgeting in her seat. She kept gazing at Suzanne worriedly, empathizing with her dilemma. As well she might. I did, too.

Finally Alison offered, "Why don't I make the calls?"

"Because one of them might recognize your voice, dear. But none of them knows what Suzanne sounds like. And besides, her French-accented English is probably just what the staff at the consulate would sound like. She sounds more . . . official . . . older."

"But," Suzanne said, "is there no other way to accomplish what you are trying to do?"

"No, I don't think so. I've got to frighten the killer to flush him out. Something dramatic like this is called for. And it has to sound authentic."

"I am not afraid, Alice," she said. "It's not that I am afraid to do it. It's only that . . . " Her voice trailed off.

I felt genuinely bad for her. But I didn't see any choice. She was the only one I could turn to now, the only one I could trust. If this didn't work, nothing would. There would be no second chance.

It's true, the scheme had come to me very quickly . . . a burst, a flash. But, sitting there waiting for Suzanne to decide, I realized how simple and foolproof it was. The kiss of death idea had wiped all the cobwebs away from my brain. Yes, this plan was sound. It *would* work. *If* Suzanne came through.

"My God," Alison mused. "All this because I was reminiscing about Hugh and Piaf."

"Well, yes and no, dear. It was your description of Piaf's kiss that made me think of another kiss. You were there when it happened.

Don't you remember? Dorothy and Ray Allen shared a long kiss after we left the plane. You poured the champagne."

Alison nodded unhappily, not fully understanding what was going on but asking no more questions.

Suzanne decisively pushed away her coffee cup and stood. "Very well," she said. "I will do it. If it is so important."

"I took her hands in mine. "Thank you, Suzanne." It was all I could say. And thankfully, it was enough for her.

Alison was at the far table, seated next to Ray Allen Penze, whose arm rested lightly on her chair. She was wearing a short velvet dress with lace at the collar. I sat near Cilla and Brian.

Sidney Rice was the first to be summoned. He groaned when the manager informed him he was wanted on the telephone. He rose and slowly made his way into the lounge. He came back five minutes later and wordlessly resumed eating. I could read nothing on his face or in his manner.

Within half an hour Ray Allen's number was up. Much the same scenario was repeated. He seemed a little wary when he took his seat again, but he mentioned nothing about the content of the call.

I noted with interest that neither of the first two "contestants" appeared to be terribly disturbed by his call. As if inquiries from a government official about bodies and autopsies were the commonest thing in the world. Maybe we had all become hardened to tragedy by now—after the shocking progression of events from the auto crash to the withdrawal of the financing to the brutal murder of Mona Columbia. What could a phone call mean to any of us now—any of us except the killer.

Claude Braque was not at the table. One of the maids had to go to his room with the message that he had a call. I saw him enter the main house, go into the lounge to talk on the phone, and a few minutes later leave again.

Brian was called just as dessert was being served. Call number four—that did it then. I didn't stay long enough to observe his manner when he rejoined the table. Instead, I feigned a headache and left, saying hasty good-byes to all. But my glance lingered on Alison, who nodded her understanding. The plan was now in place.

Once outside, I raced to the cottage, slipped into a warm coat, and then headed for the village.

I was to meet Suzanne near the café. Alison would follow as soon as she could. I sent up a prayer that the little Citroen had one more adventure left in it.

10

As Suzanne, Alison, and I made our way along the darkened roads, the Citroen coughing a little, I was thinking, of all things, of those three little school maids from Gilbert and Sullivan.

When we reached the old country hospital it was past ten. A few lights burned dimly inside the building. Nom de Dieu Hospital was made up of two long narrow buildings in the shape of a cross. At the end of the horizontal wing of the cross was a squat little edifice, something like a refrigerated garage—the morgue. It looked very much like the kind of improvised thing one would see in the Minnesota countryside . . . a temporary but quite efficient way to keep a body from decaying before the funeral. Of course, I couldn't be sure that Dorothy's body was in there.

We three maidens huddled in the old war horse of a car. They hadn't had a night this cold in years, Suzanne informed us. The Citroen had no heater.

"Where should the car sit?" Suzanne asked in her lovely way.

"Off the road, Suzanne—over there—so no one sees us."

She guided the car to a weedy shallow. We had an excellent view of the hospital, for what that was worth. There did not seem to be a soul about. We saw a couple of those little put-put vehicles, called deux chevals, in the lot, so there must have been at least a skeleton crew on duty. Perhaps in season the hospital boomed with an assortment of tourist disasters. But tonight there was nothing but an occasional ghostly shadow floating by the white-curtained windows.

"Now that we're here and hidden," Alison whispered, "what are we supposed to do?"

I knew why she was whispering: the place was spooky. And the light fog rolling in and out only bolstered that atmosphere. The windshield began to gloss over, so Suzanne opened the window. The blast of frigid wind was hard to bear.

"We're waiting for a killer," I said, addressing Alison's question. Foolishly, I was hoping that the gentleness with which I'd said it would ameliorate any panic she might feel.

"Why does the killer want to come here?"

"To prevent an autopsy's taking place. He cannot afford to have that happen."

Suzanne, having long ago understood the part her phone calls had played, nodded sagely, but asked, "How do you know that one of *them* killed Miss Dodd?"

"Believe me, it has to be one of them," I replied confidently, though in all honesty my confidence was shaky.

"Can we please have the window closed?" asked a shivering Alison. She was in the back seat, which was like a wind tunnel. Suzanne rolled up the window.

And as she was doing so, "Look under your seat," she instructed me.

"Under my seat? For what?"

"Just look."

I reached under the seat and my hand brushed against a cylindrical object. I pulled it up. Bless her heart, as my grandmother was fond of saying. I was holding one of those old-fashioned thermos bottles. I unscrewed the lid. Suzanne had prepared hot chocolate for us. Steaming. Rich. Deep. I'd never tasted any like it.

"I melt a bar of chocolate in the pan," she said when I asked her what her secret was. "Robert always said it was better than the *chocolat chaud* at Deux Magots."

"I agree with him," said Alison, draining the cup I had passed to her. "Better than the Café Flore, too."

Again I had that pang of jealousy. More things they had in common. More happy memories. They had been in the same Paris cafés with their beloved late husbands.

I felt Alison's hand on my shoulder then, gripping, clawing at my coat.

"Someone's coming!" she said, her fright evident in her voice.

She was right.

A vehicle drove past us and turned onto the hospital grounds. I peered through my window but it was hard to discern the shape of the car.

"It's the van! The one I drove from the airport."

Right again.

I felt a rush of both pride and fear. For I had been right as well. The killer had come to make sure Dorothy's body was not autopsied.

But who was in the van? It was impossible to see. The driver had by now maneuvered the van directly in front of the hospital entrance. We saw the figure emerge from the vehicle and walk toward the entrance, then suddenly redirect his steps and vanish off to one side of the building.

"He's going around back," I said. "To the morgue. Probably to see how he can get in. Then he'll pull the van around there."

"Are you going to try to stop him, Aunt Alice?"

"Certainly not."

"What *are* you—we—going to do?"

"Nothing. Sit and wait."

"This is awful," Alison said in distaste.

"Scared?" I asked.

"Yes. Maybe. But it isn't so much that. It's . . . well, how could someone kidnap a dead person? It's repulsive."

"It's easy," I said, "once you've already committed murder."

She laughed nervously. "For some reason, it almost seems worse—more obscene—to steal a dead body than to murder a living one."

"Perhaps you have lived in France too long," Suzanne quipped.

My niece leaned into the front seat and asked me urgently, "Tell us what they'll find if they do the autopsy. What is it he's trying to cover up?"

I didn't have time to explain. The driver had appeared again, coming back to the van. We watched wordlessly as he stood there. He just stood there.

Finally, Suzanne whispered exasperatedly, "For what does he wait?"

"I don't know," I said unhappily. "Maybe he's trying to decide whether to bring the van to the body or the body to the van."

"But how will he manage the coffin?" Alison asked.

"There aren't any coffins in a morgue . . . " I began. But Alison herself cut me off.

"Oh, yes, that's right. The corpses would be under simple white sheets—or in those horrific plastic bags—like a workman's lunch. How stupid of me. I had . . . forgotten."

I felt terrible for her.

Outside, the driver of the van began to stomp his feet. Due to the distance and the night, his face was still invisible.

"If he's so cold, he should get into the van and turn on the heater. It has a very good heater." Alison slipped her hands halfway out of her gloves and blew on her fingers.

The figure was circling the van now. My stomach churned and knotted. What on earth was he doing out there? And who was he? I stared into the night until my eyes ached, trying to catch just a single body or facial aspect that was familiar . . . something that I could tie to Penze or Rice, Braque or Watts. But all I knew for sure was that it was a male figure.

"Alice! He is opening the door," Suzanne whispered.

Not really. He was merely standing by the driver's door, one gloved hand on the handle. What was he waiting for? Had another vehicle entered from a path we couldn't see and dropped off a conspirator? Maybe he did have an associate, or maybe he'd paid someone at the hospital to help him remove the body.

"Smoke, Alice," said Suzanne.

"No, thanks."

"*There's smoke, Alice!* Look!"

"Where?"

I followed the direction of her pointing finger. At first it looked like fog. The fog was swirling in and out. Clearing and re-forming. But no, it wasn't fog. It was much too dark. Black now, against the black night.

He saw it too. Because, before I could even react, he was in the van, revving the engine, and the van was tearing away from the hospital driveway.

Now we could see the red tongues of flame. I knew what had happened at once. At once, but too late. It had just never occurred to me that rather than kidnap the corpse he might torch the place.

The van was almost out of sight now.

"Hurry! Both of you," I barked out. "Get in there and tell someone. And call the police!"

The moment they jumped from the Citroen and began running toward the main entrance, I slid behind the wheel.

And I panicked all over again. A car with a shift! It had been years since I'd even seen a system like that. Gram had had an old Nash Rambler out at the farm, something one of her neighbors had left her in his will.

The taillights of the gray van were vanishing into the scenery.

In my desperation, the litany came back to me. *Shift into first gear by pressing and depressing the clutch and bringing the shift down and toward you. Second gear was straight up and away from you. Third was straight down.* Yes, that was it. Enough to get me bumping out of the shadows and on the road.

Then the Citroen began to pick up speed under my urging. In another minute I could make out the shape of the van up ahead. It was heading back in the direction of Ste. Ruffin.

The driver must have spotted me, too, because he began to pick up speed. I lost him again, for a while, but the roads were so dark and rutted that the van could not go at top speed. Maybe if the vehicle were weighted with goods or people the ride would have been swifter, smoother. But with only one occupant, it was literally leaping off the road as its speed increased.

But the battle-weary Citroen was like an armor-plated lizard, swiftly slithering ahead and keeping the pressure on the van. I knew that if the other driver continued to increase his speed he'd never be able to control the van. He was going to have to slow down or crash.

I was so exhilarated that for a few moments I lost sight of the fact that I was chasing a killer, not playing a tomboy game of stock car racing.

The van bounced up high once—I flinched, steeling myself—then again. It swerved wildly and skidded. But he weathered the shock and the vehicle righted itself.

But then came a curve and the out-of-nowhere headlights of an oncoming car. The van pitched off the road, spun dizzily, and ended up perpendicular to the road, straddling it like a monster toll collector.

There was an overpowering smell of burning rubber when I jumped from the Citroen. I saw a figure slumped over the wheel of the van. Whoever it was, he was a very bad driver. And he had obviously panicked. Perhaps he'd thought the Citroen was a police vehicle. I think plainclothes police in France used to drive them. I ran a few minutes from one of those fifties policiers directed by Jean-Pierre

Melville through my memory. Yes, the police
were driving that make of car. But then, so
were the robbers.

I stopped a few feet away from the van.
What do to? I was sure Suzanne had phoned
the police, but how long would it take Inspector Lucas to get here? Suppose the van was
seconds away from exploding? Suppose the
driver was seconds away from dying, and I
could prevent that by helping him now.

I inched toward the still figure. This was
what I wanted, wasn't it? The moment I'd been
waiting for. My chance to put things together
. . . and blow the case wide open. I was just
about to bring all the elements together into a
coherent whole: a tragic auto accident on a
country road; the mysterious withdrawal of
the funding for a doomed motion picture; the
horrible murder of a talented young woman
who was even more complex and knowing
than she appeared to be; the secrets held by
an ambitious young actor with more chest
hair than principles.

So what was I waiting for?

The man behind the wheel was helpless—
what could he do to me now?

I was right outside the door of the van now.
I hesitated—for hours, it felt like—before
touching the handle. But finally I did, and
pulled the door open carefully. I was trying to
determine whether or not he was breathing.

He was.

And at the same moment I began to feel for
a pulse in his neck, he came to life. He sat

straight up in the seat, banged the door back savagely, and sent me reeling backward.

I was sprawled out in the dirt and gravel, staring up at the man.

Brian Watts loomed over me, both hands wrapped around a large gun.

"Stay where you are, Alice," he said with menacing hoarseness. "I mean it! Stay exactly where you are."

I didn't say a word. I didn't even nod to show I understood he meant what he said. My heart was going like a jackhammer in a clothes closet.

"Why are you following me? Why couldn't you just leave me alone!" he screamed out, sounding betrayed as well as angry. Brian's absolute derangement was plain now. Maybe setting the fire had unhinged him. Or maybe the wild car chase had done it. But he was clearly over the edge now. And he looked as if he might pull that trigger at any second.

He was raking in air, his chest heaving with the effort. Even with both his hands around the weapon, it was trembling and rattling. I never took my eyes off the barrel.

But then, eventually, he seemed to calm. "You know I killed Dorothy, don't you?" he said, almost placid now.

"Yes, Brian. I do know." And no sooner were the words out of my mouth than I realized what a stupid thing I'd just done. Here was a desperate man—and a nervous one at that—holding me at gunpoint in the middle of nowhere. For all I knew, he thought I was acting alone and had told no one I suspected him. Hell, in a way he was right. For all I knew, he was calculating that he could kill me, too—and get away with it. And what do I do but admit I know he's a murderer!

Nestleton's Greatest Cases, indeed. I seem to have this way of backing into the truth of a thing. And it so often turns out to be a rusty nail.

But my admission had the odd effect of calming him even more. He actually lowered the gun a bit.

Then he said in a wistful voice, almost a whine, "Oh, Alice. You just don't understand. I didn't mean to kill her. I meant only to cripple. Why would I kill her and take her out of it all? Death is peace. No, I wanted her to suffer every day, day after day. I wanted her to know what it was like to live crippled. Like me. Because that's what prison did to me. And she put me there."

He stepped back, away from me. But when I tried getting to my feet, he warned, "Stay! Stay where you are."

I remained as I was, arms and legs out, hurting.

Brian took one of his hands away from the gun and waved it in the air in a gesture of despair.

"Too bad, isn't it, Alice?" he said sadly. "It would have been nice if you and I could have been friends. We *were* friends, after a fashion though, weren't we? I liked you the very first time we met. Remember, Alice? Remember the first time we met—in that lovely Chinese restaurant in New York?"

"Yes, Brian. I remember it very clearly." I was trying to speak soothingly. But I needn't have bothered. I don't think he was listening at all. He appeared to be turning things over in his mind, speculating, musing.

No, he wasn't listening. He was *smiling*. And he was still smiling when he lifted the gun and placed it against his ear.

"Don't . . . *do* that, Brian," I choked out. "Please don't—"

The gun exploded in the still black night and he crumpled almost simultaneously with the blast.

I quite literally crawled over to where he lay, screaming with every inch of progress I made. I knew at once that Brian Watts was dead. The bullet had shattered his skull. The ground was a pond of blood and tissue.

I went on screaming, but I don't know for how long.

I was quiet by the time Inspector Lucas arrived. He and Suzanne and Alison. Then the other police vehicles and eventually the ambulance. Soon I was in a circle of flashing lights and caring arms. Lucas took me over to his car and helped me onto the front seat. I felt a rush of warm air from the heater and then Suzanne appeared with a blanket and a pair of gloves.

Lucas pulled out a small silver flask and poured me a thimbleful of the liquid from it.

"What is this?" I asked.

"Armagnac," Lucas said. "It's . . . medicinal."

I drank it down and burst into crazy-sounding laughter. "It's just," I tried explaining, "all those last reels, all those movies. I can't keep it straight whether it's a Belmondo picture . . . or *The Third Man* . . . or *Hill Street Blues*." My body shook.

"You probably should not try to speak yet, Alice," Suzanne offered.

"Ah, yes," Lucas said solicitously. "That would probably be ideal. Except that there are some matters about which Madame Nestleton must talk, I fear. There seem to be a few things I have not been told—*n'est-ce pas*, madame?"

I nodded, feeling more in control now. I was frightened and weary but I knew I had to tell him what I knew, or thought I knew, about the dead Brian Watts.

"What I'm going to tell you, Inspector Lucas, is not gospel. I don't know the whole story on the two murders and the suicide that have occurred over these last days.

"But I know quite a bit. For the story to make sense, I'll have to go back to the mid-1980s, when Dorothy Dodd owned, and then folded a prestigious magazine in—"

Lucas held up one hand and interrupted my narrative, "What is this 'folded'?"

"Looted, bankrupted, defrauded . . . " I floundered. "Suzanne, can you manage to explain it?"

She obliged in what I took to be colloquial French.

Lucas offered me another drink and I eagerly accepted.

I continued. "Ms. Dodd owned and published a magazine in Canada. After she had looted the company and the business failed, two of her executives were indicted on fraud and embezzlement charges. They were tried, convicted, and sent to prison. Brian Watts was one of those men. Years later, after he'd served his prison term, he became associated with her again. This time as a film producer. He must have pretended to have overcome any bitterness he had toward Ms. Dodd for leaving him holding . . . well, how can I say it?"

"Yes, yes," Lucas said. "Holding the bag. I know this expression."

"Right. Well, anyway, Brian must have pretended to forgive her, but obviously his hatred for Dorothy was still very much alive—festering. Either he convinced her to back this film vehicle, *The Emptying,* for her young lover or it was something she approached him to do. I don't really know.

"He planned everything carefully. He wanted to cripple her so that she would suffer as he had in prison. But he miscalculated and she died.

"He would soon learn that he'd made another mistake. That Dorothy had anticipated danger and left instructions withdrawing all funds for the movie if anything happened to her.

"Somehow, somewhere, Mona Columbia found out about the whole plot. And she was murdered as well."

"That is all very interesting," Inspector Lucas noted. "But can you tell me by what method Madame Dodd was murdered—given the circumstances of her death? Have you any proof for your story?"

"The proof went up in smoke when the body in that morgue was burned. That's why Brian Watts tried to destroy the morgue. He thought there was going to be an autopsy, that Dorothy's family was demanding one."

"Why did he think this?"

I wanted to look at Suzanne for quick confirmation that it would be best not to disclose how Brian had come to think there was going to be an autopsy. But I didn't dare meet her eyes for fear Lucas would notice the exchange of glances.

"It's a long story, Inspector," I said dismissively. "We don't have the time."

"Time, madame? The time for what?"

"To confront Ray Allen Penze, Ms. Dodd's lover. He was the accomplice in the murder."

"In which murder? Madame Dodd's or Mademoiselle Columbia's?"

"Unquestionably the first. I'm not sure about the second."

"And when he is—what did you say?—'confronted,' Monsieur Penze will reveal the baffling way in which Madame Dodd's murder was carried out?"

I thought his words were perhaps becoming tinged with a measure of sarcasm.

"I think he will," I said.

"And I think, Madame Nestleton, that you are a woman with a very strong imagination."

There seemed little doubt now about the sarcasm. But still, he was regarding me with a great deal of compassion. "Perhaps it would be well to continue our talk in the morning."

A few minutes later the inspector was driving me back to the inn. Alison and Suzanne followed in the Citroen.

I felt absolutely recharged. The shock of Brian's suicide had receded. My trembling had ceased and I no longer felt that deathly chill all over my body. I was like a wounded lynx seeking sanctuary on higher ground, and I was very close to the top and I would make it to the top if I kept moving. Ray Allen Penze was the summit. He had always been that—the center of the whole mess—whether willingly or unwillingly. I didn't know which. But I was going to find out. We all were.

We pulled up to the darkened hotel. And immediately I began confabulating another movie denouement:

A sinister black police car arrives at the hideout of a notorious killer. It is a silent moonless night. The hunted criminal is asleep inside a decrepit cabin. Cut to sleeping figure with a three-day growth of beard. Propped up next to his straw pallet is an oversize machine gun. We hear animal sounds: snarling. Cut to the maws of two highly trained, lethal-looking Dobermans standing guard on the collapsed front porch of the cabin. Cut to tension-filled faces of muscle-bound cops inside their vehicle. The dogs begin to yap loudly. Killer's eyes open suddenly. Another angle: overripe blonde in satin nightdress looking terrified as killer's hand locks around her mouth.

Well, the reality of the situation was a sight less dramatic than that. We knocked politely on the door to Ray Allen's cottage and in a few minutes the rumpled actor appeared in the doorway. He was wearing deep green silk pajama bottoms, his toned, muscular chest bare.

Neither Lucas nor I spoke while Ray Allen stood there massaging the sleep from his eye. Finally he focused on us. "What the hell is this?"

I looked past his shoulder and saw one of the Abyssinians sitting atop the pile of his packed valises in a corner of the room.

"I am Inspector Henri Lucas," my companion announced, "from the prefecture of police in Arles. I . . . we must speak with you, Monsieur Penze, on a matter of importance."

Ray Allen stepped aside wordlessly and Lucas and I went in.

"Well," Ray Allen said as he searched the top of the bureau for his cigarettes, "what is it? What's happened now?"

"Monsieur Penze," Lucas began, less assured now. "There has been . . . that is, a very unfortunate thing has just happened to Monsieur—"

Fool! No! Those words were racing through my mind. Lucas, that archetypically French gentleman, was going to blow this case. *Please, Inspector Lucas, shut up!*

But of course he could not hear my thoughts, and so kept talking. I had to take matters into my own hands, and quickly. Or Ray Allen was going to slip away.

I interrupted brazenly: "Listen, Ray Allen, there's no point in beating around the bush here. Lucas is trying to trick you. The truth is, Brian has been arrested. He's given a confession that implicates you in Dorothy's murder. You're in tremendous trouble and you'd better get an attorney for yourself."

That was all I said. Apparently it was enough.

Penze exploded in rage while the speechless inspector looked on in astonishment. Ray Allen cleared the top of a nearby bookcase with one violent sweep. The three cats ran every which way.

"That bastard! That lying son of a bitch!" The spat-out epithets seemed to take all the wind out of Ray Allen. He sat down heavily on the bed. "Jesus—I knew it, I knew it," he muttered hopelessly.

"I think you'd better tell us—the inspector—what happened, Ray Allen. The whole story."

He looked up and nodded slowly, but, instead of directing his words to Lucas, maintained eye contact with me.

"Okay. Okay. I'll tell you how it happened. You know what I was, don't you? Dorothy's lap dog, Dorothy's . . . thing. It was like my job, to escort her, play the stud. Yeah, she gave me a lot, but not for free. Nothing was free with Dot. But that was okay. I was hungry and the career was going nowhere fast. And she could do a lot for me."

The cats came wandering back in at that moment. Ray Allen seemed to be studying them. "Yes, everything was going along okay. Then I met Mona. At first I thought it was just going to be another piece on the side. Hell, I couldn't be expected not to look at another woman again for the rest of my life. Not even Dot would expect that—as long as it was discreet and as long as it was temporary.

"But it wasn't a temporary thing with Mona. I fell in love with her. Dot didn't know who I was seeing, but she was beginning to suspect it might be serious. *Might be*—Mona was the only one I ever gave a damn about since I was twelve years old and in love with my gym teacher's wife."

He laughed ruefully then. The muscles in his chest and arms rippled. I was suddenly struck by what a handsome young man he was. And I was also aware that Inspector Lucas had quietly shifted his position in the room, as if blocking the door, and as if freeing his arms if he needed to draw a weapon.

"People were starting to talk about it," Penze continued, his voice now frozen in a monotone. "And then that idiot Brian found out about it. He showed up at Mona's hotel in New York while I was there. Said he had an idea for getting Dorothy out of the way for the first ten days or so of shooting. He said it would be a boon to the whole company to have her out of the picture because he knew she'd interfere every step of the way. And Mona and I would benefit the most, because we could have ten days together here. Mona's cover would be that she was doing an article on the film. It sounded almost too good to be true.

"Brian had a plan. A 'brilliant' plan. He knew Dot had this crazy thing with her health—she was a hypochondriac. I knew it, too. She was forever complaining about every disease or germ or virus under the sun. Hell, she'd already had two of those treatments in Switzerland, where they give you all new blood and stuff to get the impurities out of your system. She took sleep cures and millions of vitamins— all kinds of things. Well, Brian said he had a surefire way to get her to check herself into a hospital the moment we arrived in France. To hear him tell it, she was probably going to get on the next plane to go to her doctor in Paris."

He stopped talking then, abruptly, and looked around with hard eyes. He stared for a long time at Inspector Lucas, perhaps attempting to evaluate how deeply his monologue was implicating him in Lucas's eyes.

I didn't want Ray Allen to stop talking, though. I had to keep his monologue going.

"That's a very touching story, Ray Allen. But don't you think it's about time we cut to the chase? I mean, how you did it. I'm talking about the kiss, Ray Allen . . . the kiss."

He cocked his head like a dog listening to some far-off sound. He shifted the position of his arms, folding them.

Inspector Lucas's puzzlement was total. "The *kiss*, did you say?"

I ignored him and honed in on Ray Allen again. "That kiss at the airport," I said. "That was how you murdered her."

It was my use of the term "murder" that spurred him on. He shook his head violently. "Stop saying that! It was *not* a murder. Back in New York, Brian gave me a small glassine vial. Like the ones actors keep in their mouths during a fight scene. When you take a punch you're supposed to bleed. In modern movies, anyway. They want it to look realistic. So you just crush the vial between your teeth and the fake blood oozes out. Brian told me there was nothing in that vial but a common diuretic and something to give her mild stomach cramps. That's all. He told me to kiss Dot when the plane landed and break the thing. He said make it a passionate kiss, make it look good, like I was just so happy to be here and starting the picture. It was supposed to be harmless, don't you see? Dorothy would have run to the hospital thinking her kidneys were going or something. She would've ordered every test known to mankind. And meanwhile she'd be out of everybody's hair. What's so bad about that, huh? That sound like a murder to you?"

His eyes were wild now, his voice tremulous. "But it wasn't what Brian had said it was. That was no diuretic that I transferred to Dorothy when we kissed. It was acid or something. Some kind of hallucinogen. I realized it only a few minutes after we got into the van. I felt all kinds of crazy things going on in my head, but I knew how to handle it. Dorothy didn't, and I was afraid she was going to kill us all. But she didn't. She just wound up killing herself. What was I supposed to do? Tell?

"Then Mona showed up. When she found out how it had all gone wrong, she was sick with fear at my involvement. She begged me to go to the police, but I wouldn't. She said we'd all wind up in trouble if I didn't do something. But I just couldn't."

Ray Allen stood up suddenly, and Lucas and I tensed.

Penze was almost incoherent now. "She must have gone to him," he cried out.

"Who do you mean, Ray Allen?" I asked gently.

"Mona! Mona! She must have gone to Brian. Told him she knew what had happened. I know she was trying to protect me in some way. Maybe she tried to make him confess and clear me. I don't know. But knowing Mona, she must have told him what she knew, told him he couldn't get away with it. And that has to be why he killed her!" He broke into sobs then, and when he finally straightened himself again, he shouted, "I hope they put that bastard's head on the block for what he did to my baby. And I'm going to be there laughing."

"Are you so sure it was Brian who killed her?"

"Of course he did. He's crazy, I tell you. Who else but that crazy bastard would do such a thing?"

"Perhaps you, Ray Allen," I responded matter-of-factly.

He leapt toward me, grasping the top of my blouse with one hand and then, unable to maintain his balance, fell backward onto the floor, ripping half the garment away. "I loved her! Don't you understand that, you stupid, meddling—"

It was then that Inspector Lucas drew his weapon. Ray Allen's tantrum suddenly ceased. "Monsieur Penze," Lucas said distinctly, "you will please dress yourself. We will be traveling to Arles."

I stared down at my ripped blouse. It had been a lovely, vintage Willy Smith, wine-red, shiny buttons up the front.

There came an insistent knocking on the door of the cottage. Inspector Lucas turned and admitted Suzanne and Alison, who both wore alarmed expressions.

There was a sudden scrabbling sound from across the room. We all turned toward it. But it was not Ray Allen Penze attempting an escape. The source of the noise was Maud/Piaf, who had scrambled off the mantel and was racing across the room. In a single bound, she leapt up into Alison's arms and lovingly nuzzled her forehead.

Another kind of bad movie would have Piaf

break into a few choruses of "Je Ne Regrette Rien" just about now. I waited for the opening chords. But all I heard was the everyday kind of purring of a contented cat.

Suzanne helped me to my room.

So now I knew how Dorothy Dodd had been killed. I believed Brian Watts wanted merely to cripple her, not to kill. And I believed that Ray Allen Penze thought there was a mild diuretic in that vial, rather than a powerful hallucinogenic drug. As for who killed Mona Columbia, well, I just didn't know. But I had accomplished what I set out to do. And I was exhausted.

I lay down, still wearing the torn blouse, and fell asleep the minute my head hit the lacy pillow. No dreams that night. No memories. No delusions. No regrets.

There was sunshine all around the edges of the curtain. I sat up, feeling good, and saw Suzanne on the rocking chair, where she had spent the night. Alison had slept beside me, with Bushy. As for Pancho, it was the usual: whereabouts unknown.

"How are you feeling?" Suzanne asked.

"All new," I said.

Alison stretched lazily. "Morning . . . I'm hungry, Aunt Alice." She sounded very much like a little girl, and looked the part, too, her pretty hair all tangled.

"I think we should all go to the inn right now and get breakfast. It's like we're on a camping trip," I said. I threw a sweater over an old T-shirt and the three of us marched toward the dining room where hot coffee and warm croissants were lying next to pots of wild raspberry jam.

We never got that coffee.

An ear-splitting explosion stunned us. Suddenly people were running out of the inn and the cottages—staff and guests.

A pale-faced Suzanne pointed toward the village. We saw a single fireball rise into the air as if it were being belched out by some subterranean demon.

"The old church!" Suzanne began to run. "It's near the old church."

Alison and I hesitated for only a second. Then we sped off as well. The fireball had vanished and in its place ugly black smoke was swirling up and then to the west.

In a few minutes we reached the church wall and turned the corner.

Exactly where Dorothy Dodd had crashed into the wall, now there was another vehicle.

Only this one had exploded on contact and burned. It must have been traveling at a much greater rate of speed.

We slowed our pace, approaching the scene tentatively, as one would approach an open grave.

There were traces of red on the hulk. Blood? No, paint. Red paint.

It had been a red car.

I sank to one knee, suddenly aware of the enormity of what I was seeing.

It was Mona Columbia's red Triumph that had torn into that wall. The car the police had been unable to find.

The charred corpse in the front seat looked like a mannequin—a grotesque parody of a car safety demonstration.

I didn't want to know who it was. But I did know.

Suzanne said quietly to Alison, "Stay here with your aunt," and she walked forward.

Alison held on to me tightly, as if I were some kind of invalid, but I did not mind.

Suzanne walked back toward us in a normal gait, but her face was grim. Her glance went from side to side, as though she were searching for wildflowers. But this was winter in the Camargue.

"It is Cilla Hood," she said simply.

Yes, it *would* be Cilla. I knew what had happened: Cilla had only been trying to do her usual job of tidying up after Brian. Clearing the path for him. Ridding him of the thorn in his paw—the young woman who could send him back to prison. Cilla must have loved Brian Watts very much. Perhaps she hadn't even told him that it was she who had crushed the pretty film critic's skull. Perhaps it had been an anonymous love offering.

But what had Brian Watts ever given her— emotionally, financially, or any other way— that would elicit such idiotic, annihilating devotion? I didn't know. I didn't know.

And then the worst fate of all. The man whose freedom Cilla thought she had saved by compromising her own had blown his own head off.

What was she to do then? She retrieved the car she had hidden, got behind the wheel, and drove it at top speed into the wall where the bloody chain of waste and murder had begun.

I hadn't known or understood Cilla Hood any better than I had Mona Columbia—much less, in fact. Even so, I found I had a few tears for her, too.

France was a bad place for Nestletons, I had told Alison bitterly. I told her I was taking her home with me, to New York. I also made her understand that she would never get Piaf back legitimately. Maud/Piaf—no matter what you called her—belonged to Dorothy Dodd's heirs now.

And there was no doubt in anyone's mind that Dorothy's cats would be cared for with love by Dorothy's heirs. Who, anyway, would abuse a multimillion-dollar media darling? Or her sisters? There was also a good chance that once all humans and cats were back in the U.S., Alison would be able to visit Piaf. They could sing duets . . . with no regrets.

Alison did understand about the cat. However, she was sad that my experience in France, my very first trip to Europe, had turned out so horribly. She wanted at least to show me Paris. And, after all, I had a few dollars left from the advance I'd received—enough to finance a wonderful brief holiday for us. Also, I'd be fulfilling the promise I'd made to Bushy that he was going to be a genuine Parisian cat, if only for a few days. We decided to rent a car and wind our way leisurely into the City of Light, cats and all.

It wasn't to be.

Late that night, my agent phoned from New York. The news of the ill-fated film had been picked up by the international press— "Slaughter on Set of Frog Murder Pic" was the way the trade papers were headlining the story—and it seemed I was suddenly, in my agent's words, "hot as hell." Ira Levin was ready with a new Off Broadway thriller, and the director wanted *me*. Now.

Suzanne was disappointed as well. Disappointed that we were all parting so soon and that I would not be able to salvage the trip with a Paris fling. But she cheerfully offered us a lift to the Marseilles airport. The little Citroen still had the necessary juice.

It was disturbing. As the plane took off I felt that I was bringing home with me the remains of Dorothy Dodd and Brian Watts and Mona Columbia *and* Cilla Hood. Even though there wasn't a single coffin on board—not even an urn.

It was the stewardess who got me back into reality.

"Excuse me? Aren't you in the movies?" she asked as she set down our complimentary drinks.

"No," I said. But then I amended that. "Well, I used to be."

BE SURE TO CATCH
THE NEXT
ALICE NESTLETON
MYSTERY,

*A CAT
ON THE
CUTTING EDGE*
COMING TO YOU
FROM SIGNET IN
NOVEMBER 1994.

1

I never had any problem cutting my Maine Coon cat's claws. Following the advice of another cat lover I knew, I would merely sneak up on Bushy when he was sleeping and clip one nail before he knew what was happening. For every snooze he took, he lost a sharp claw. At the end of the afternoon—*voilà!*—he had a manicure.

But Pancho, my lunatic half-tailed refugee from the ASPCA, was another matter. He never slept. At least he never slept while I was awake. So, a few times a year, I had to dump him into the carrier and take him to the vet to perform the honors.

Now Pancho, even though he spent his entire day fleeing from imaginary enemies, was always very easy to get into his carrier and no problem at all once inside of it. In fact, he seemed to enjoy the whole process—that is, until we arrived at the vet's office and he saw the dreaded clippers in the doctor's hand.

The only thing I had to do was to bribe him with a little saffron rice, fed to him just before I dumped him into the carrier. For some reason beyond human comprehension, Pancho loved saffron rice with a passion.

So, that's what I did on that Tuesday afternoon in April. I gave him a small bowl of saffron rice and waited until he had annihilated the offering, smacking his lips. Then I opened his battered old carrier, a top loader, and picked him up.

To put it mildly, all hell broke loose. Pancho went ballistic. First he tensed. Then, as I started to push him into the box, he began to struggle. I held on tighter, he struggled more. I warned him, tapping him on the nose. Then he became a wildcat and I just couldn't hold him.

"What is the matter with you?" I demanded. "You always liked your carrier." He sat down about ten feet away from me and eyed me balefully. I approached him slowly. He didn't run.

But the moment I picked him up he started to fight again. And I lost my temper and I fought back, and he started to screech and I started to yell. Then I felt a sharp stab of pain on my forearm and I dropped him.

Pancho had bloodied me! I couldn't believe it. I sat down on a chair and almost wept.

"How could you do that, Pancho?" I implored. He looked totally unconcerned. I searched for Bushy for spiritual help, but my Maine Coon had vanished.

It was a very bad time for this to happen. Things had definitely not been going my way as of late. My niece, Alison Chevigny, with whom I had been brought together so wonderfully and unexpectedly in France during my unsuccessful fling at cinematic stardom, was head over heels in love. And after staying with me for six months, she had decided to go off and live with the man. She was moving out and I knew I would miss her.

In addition, the featured role I had been promised in an upcoming Broadway sleuther had evaporated when the producer met me and realized I was the same actress he'd wrestled with—and lost—ten years ago.

In addition, one of my very best cat-sitting clients, Mrs. Ridout, was moving to Charlotte, North Carolina, with her husband, Jock, and their cat, Reggie.

In addition, the part I had been offered in the production of a TV movie about the prison life of the woman who murdered the famous Scarsdale diet doctor was written out of the script at the last moment. I had really been counting on that money. Was there any other sane reason to have accepted the role in the first place?

And to make matters even worse, my special

friend, Tony Basillio, had been acting very strangely lately, accusing me of infidelity and various other crimes.

Oh yes, it was a bad time for me, a bad time for Pancho to have become so aggressive, a very bad time indeed.

I tried to reason with the gray cat, who was now half hidden under one end of the sofa, ready to make a run for the hallway if I approached.

"Pancho, I want you to listen to me now. Sooner or later you're going to have to get your nails clipped. And for that to happen I have to get you to the vet. And to do that I have to put you in your box, Pancho. It's a routine we've followed many times— right? . . . Isn't that right, Pancho? So why this sudden antagonism toward that carrier? What is going on with you, old friend?"

But he would not be swayed by reason. I realized that the only way I'd get him into the box was to knock him unconscious. And I was not prepared to do that.

I glared at him. He slouched lower and glared back. We were obviously experiencing one of those very rare and very malevolent failures to communicate.

Wearily, I went to the phone and dialed Dr. Leon, my new vet, who had come recommended by John Cerise, an old friend and the most knowledgeable cat man I know. Leon's practice was down in the Village—not my neighborhood but only ten minutes away by cab. Peg Oates, his assistant, took my call. When she heard I wanted to cancel the appointment, she switched me to Dr. Leon.

"Dr. Leon, it's Alice Nestleton. I'm sorry to mess up your schedule this afternoon, but I can't get my cat into his carrier."

"Don't worry," he said in his kindly voice, "we'll reschedule when kitty is up to it."

I liked Dr. Leon. I had seen him only three times, twice with Bushy and once with Pancho, and each time he had impressed me more, particularly when we thought that Bushy had a serious pancreatic deficiency. He told Bushy and me exactly what he was going to do each step of the way and why he was doing it.

"I'm searching for the byproduct enzyme Trypsin," he had said as he ordered the tests. "If it's not there, then it has to be put there, or Bushy will not be able to digest and absorb food properly."

Leon was a short, powerfully built man in his late thirties and he just seemed to scoop his patients up, preparatory to working his healing magic.

Just as I was about to hang up, Dr. Leon asked, "Did you ever hear of the Village Cat People?"

I couldn't help laughing at the name. It sounded like the cult following for a bad Hollywood movie. Or the title of the movie itself.

Then I got myself under control. "Sorry," I said, "it's just that the name is so funny. No, Dr. Leon, I've never heard of the Village Cat People. Who are they?"

"A group of veterinary technicians who make house calls. A sort of feline EMS. Full service. They're not vets, but close enough for what they do."

"House calls?"

"Sure. They'll come to your home and tranquilize your cat. Or corral him and transport him. Or do anything short of actual veterinary diagnosis and treatment."

"How ingenious," I said. What a shame I hadn't known about the Village Cat People before.

Dr. Leon gave me their phone number. I wrote it down and then asked, "Are they expensive?"

"Very reasonable."

"Then please let the appointment stand, Dr. Leon. Only make it an hour or so later. I'll call the Village Cat People and have them come here and give Pancho something to get him in hand. Then I'll bring him over."

"They can also clip his nails," Dr. Leon said.

For a moment I was put out. Didn't he want to do the clipping? I always considered that a kind of honor. "Well, I'd prefer you do it. Pancho already knows you."

"Okay. Fine. I'll be expecting you," he confirmed.

I hung up and called the Village Cat People. The pleasant-sounding woman at the other end of the line took down all the necessary information on me and the reluctant patient, Pancho. It was all handled most professionally, not at all the way an outfit with a kind of whimsical, post-hippie name like Village Cat People might have dealt with the situation. The VCP representative quoted a price for the visit and the tranquilizing injection. I agreed. She told me that one of her associates, Martha Lorenz, would arrive at my apartment within the hour.

I was greatly relieved, almost giddy. Imagine, a professional Pancho mover would be here shortly.

Then Alison came in, wondering why I was looking so disarranged. I explained what had happened. She didn't seem truly interested in my little cat problem, though. But I suppose that's the way it is when you're in love; nothing else really counts. And Alison was definitely in love. Hugely. Almost like a schoolgirl. But Alison was no schoolgirl. She was twenty-four, a grown woman who'd been married and widowed during her time in France. And now she had found love again. I knew she had it bad when she cut off all her beautiful golden hair. Only a woman in love cuts her hair that radically.

"Any calls?" she asked sweetly, going into the kitchen to put the kettle on. Alison drank a great deal of coffee. As did I. But she'd brought in her own fancy coffeepot months ago, chastising me heavily for my instant coffee fetish.

Any calls? That meant, of course, Had *he* called? *He* being one Felix Drinnan, a fifty-one-year-old psychiatrist, who had more money than God, both from his practice and his family, and who seemed to be as in love with Alison as she was with him. He owned and lived in an entire four-story house in the West Village, on Barrow Street. I didn't dislike him, but I couldn't say I liked him, either. And I found it strange that Alison would fall in love with a man old enough to be her father. Someone who collected ancient coins and antique quilts. After all, her late husband, Hugh Chevigny, had been much closer to her own age, and he had been a gifted cat trainer. Well, it was stupid to make comparisons, but the whole thing confused me and made me unhappy.

I poked my head into the small kitchen. "Felix didn't call," I said. "But to be honest, I was so upset about what was happening with Pancho that the phone might have rung without my even hearing it."

"Understandable, Aunt Alice," she said, sweetly again. Alison was becoming positively nieceish—if any such word exists.

Then she asked, "What time are those people coming over?"

"What people?"

"The ones you just told me about. The cat people."

"Oh, no, that's their collective name. Only one person is coming. I think her name is Marjorie Lorenz . . . no, Martha Lorenz."

"Shall I stay and help you?"

"How are you going to help?" I retorted, a bit caustically, as if in all the time she had been with me she had not helped me at all. Which was untrue. She had helped me in every way possible.

"Well, Aunt Alice, if Pancho is determined not to be caught, it might take more than you and the cat person to catch him and give him that shot."

"Really, Alison, you needn't worry. Miss Lorenz does things like this for a living. We'll be okay."

She poured coffee into each of two mugs on the counter. She was making a cup for me without even asking. For some reason that irritated me. It seemed condescending. She mixed it properly, a little less than half a cup for me, then a third of a Sweet 'n Low packet. Tony Basillio had once told me that I drink coffee like his uncle from the old country. Now, that I took as a compliment.

Alison handed me my coffee. We stayed together in the kitchen while we drank. She held her cup to warm her palms, as though it were wintertime and there was no heat in the apartment.

"You know," she mused, "I really thought I would never be in love again. I mean, after Hugh killed himself, the idea of having anything to do with another man seemed so remote . . . absurd . . . impossible. And now here I am, thousands of miles away from Hugh—from his grave—all those memories . . . and all I can think of is Felix. Hugh seems like some sort of. . . ." She didn't finish the sentence.

Had she wanted to involve me in a discussion of one's responsibility to the dead? Of what constitutes loyalty to their memory? I didn't know what she was talking about, really. Maybe she was just talking. Maybe she was a bit frightened about making the move.

"Though sometimes I do call Felix, Hugh," she said, sounding a little bitter.

"It's a common thing," I said soothingly.

"Not when you're making love."

I was saved from further discussion by the low throb of the street door buzzer. "The cat people are upon us," Alison said in a conspiratorial whisper.

I buzzed the cat person in and then stepped outside the apartment into the hallway to await her ascent. It was standard procedure for people in my building, because one could easily identify the climber by leaning out over the railing and looking down on the landings below. If it was one of the criminal element, one just ran back into the apartment and called 911. It wasn't that the neighborhood was crime-ridden; it wasn't. The problem was Bellevue, the massive city hospital, and its enormous network of outpatient clinics that support alcoholics, drug addicts, released mental patients, and so many other unfortunates. These people tended to wander, and show up in strange hallways.

"She's still ringing," I heard Alison call from inside the apartment.

"Please buzz her in again. The door's probably stuck. It happens from time to time."

Alison buzzed for a long time, but the bell in the apartment kept ringing and I saw no one climbing the stairs. It must be that wretched door again. And if it was stuck, it had to be opened from the inside.

"I'll go down," I told Alison.

As I descended, I silently, and then not so silently cursed Pancho as the cause of all this nonsense. It was the last time that cat would ever see any saffron rice in his little yellow bowl. I felt positively vengeful.

When I reached the bottom landing I could see the woman's figure behind the clouded glass of the door. Yes, it was obviously stuck. She was still ringing and Alison was still buzzing back. It was like a bumble bee concerto with two psychotic conductors. I just hoped I could get the door open and put an end to all the racket.

I did manage to open it. What a beautiful

young woman, I thought as I looked into Martha Lorenz's very pale eyes. Perhaps Pancho will be smitten.

But she did not step inside.

I smiled reassuringly at her. Then she pitched forward, her hands brushing against my body as she fell to the floor. I did not scream until I saw that her throat had been slit.

ENTER THE
MYSTERIOUS WORLD OF
ALICE NESTLETON IN
HER LYDIA ADAMSON
SERIES . . . BY READING
THESE OTHER
PURR-FECT
CAT CAPERS FROM SIGNET

A CAT IN A GLASS HOUSE

Brian Watts, a producer, wants Alice Nestleton to star in a French movie. This could be the big break Alice has been waiting for. Just as they have settled down with some hot tea at a favorite Chinese restaurant to discuss the details, three men walk in and kill their waitress. The restaurant is shut down by the police and Alice becomes obsessed with finding the red tabby that was in the restaurant the night of the murder. Alice is sure the missing cat and the murder are connected and she sets out to find that connection, partly to satisfy her own feline curiosity and partly to impress Sonny Hoving, the incredibly good looking police officer who's on the case.

A CAT BY ANY OTHER NAME

A hot New York summer has Alice Nestleton taking a hiatus from the stage and joining a coterie of cat-lovers in cultivating a Manhattan herb garden. When one of the cozy group plunges to her death, Alice is stunned and grief-stricken by the apparent suicide of her close friend. But aided by her two cats, she soon smells a rat. And with the help of her own felinelike instincts, Alice unravels the trail of clues and sets a trap that leads her from the Brooklyn Botanical Gardens right to her own backyard. Could the victim's dearest friends have been her own worst enemies?

A CAT IN THE WINGS

Cats, Christmas, and crime converge when Alice Nestleton finds herself on the prowl for the murderer of a once world-famous, ballet dancer. Alice's close friend has been charged with the crime and it is up to Alice to discover the truth. From Manhattan's meanest streets to the elegant salons of wealthy art patrons, Alice is drawn into a dark and dangerous web of deception, until one very special cat brings Alice the clues she needs to track down the murderer of one of the most imaginative men the ballet world has ever known.

A CAT WITH A FIDDLE

Alice Nestleton's latest job requires her to drive a musician's cat up to rural Massachusetts. Hurt by bad reviews of her latest play, Alice looks forward to a long restful weekend. But though the woods are beautiful and relaxing, Alice must share the artists' colony with a world-famous quartet beset by rivalries. Her peaceful vacation is shattered when the handsome lady-killer of a pianist turns up murdered. Alice may have a tin ear, but she has a sharp eye for suspects and a nose for clues. Her investigations lead her from the scenic Berkshire mountains to New York City, but it takes the clue of a rare breed of cat for Alice to piece together the puzzle. Alice has a good idea "whodunit," but the local police won't listen so our intrepid cat-lady is soon baiting a dangerous trap for a killer.

A CAT IN THE MANGER

Alice Nestleton, an off-off Broadway actress-turned-amateur sleuth, is crazy about cats, particularly her Maine coon, Bushy, and alley cat, Pancho. Alice plans to enjoy a merry little Christmas peacefully cat-sitting at a gorgeous Long Island estate, where she expects to be greeted by eight howling Himalayans. Instead, she stumbles across a grisly corpse. Alice has unwittingly become part of a deadly game of high-stakes horse racing, sinister seduction, and missing money. Alice knows she'll have to count on her catlike instincts and (she hopes!) nine lives to solve the murder mystery.

$2.00 REBATE!
Buy
A CAT WITH NO REGRETS
and two other Alice Nestleton mysteries and get $2.00 back.

Look for these other Alice Nestleton mysteries

A CAT IN THE MANGER
0-451-16787-2
$3.99 ($4.99 in Canada)

A CAT IN WOLF'S CLOTHING
0-451-17085-7
$3.99 ($5.50 in Canada)

A CAT BY ANY OTHER NAME
0-451-17231-0
$3.99 ($5.50 in Canada)

A CAT WITH A FIDDLE
0-451-17586-7
$3.99 ($4.99 in Canada)

A CAT IN THE WINGS
0-451-17336-8
$3.99 ($4.99 in Canada)

A CAT IN THE GLASS HOUSE
0-451-17706-1
$3.99 ($4.99 in Canada)

A CAT OF A DIFFERENT COLOR
0-451-16955-7
$3.99 ($4.99 in Canada)

TO GET THE $2.00 REBATE:

mail this certificate, the original dated sales register receipt for purchase of
A CAT WITH NO REGRETS plus purchase of at least two other
ALICE NESTLETON MYSTERIES with prices circled on the register receipt
and write the UPC numbers (from back of books below)

UPC#'s _____ _____ _____

Send to:
ALICE NESTLETON $2.00 REBATE
P.O. Box 1203 Grand Rapids, MN 55745-1203

NAME_____

ADDRESS_____APT.#_____

CITY_____STATE_____ZIP_____

⊘ SIGNET

Offer expires July 31, 1994/Mail received until August 12, 1994

This certificate must accompany your request. No duplicates accepted. Void where prohibited, taxed or restricted. Allow 4-6 weeks for shipment of rebate. Offer good only in U.S., Canada and its territories.